The Last Reef

The Last Reef

stories

Gareth L Powell

ELASTIC
PRESS

Thanks to Jetse de Vries, Andrew Hook, Andy Cox, Dan Hollifield, Leigh Dragoon, Robert Starr, Arthur Smith, Mike Gallant, Arkadiusz Nakoniecznik, Angelos Mastorakis, Keith Brooke, Mark Watson, and The Friday Flash Fictioneers.

Special thanks also to my family, especially my wife Becky, who put a lot of work into critiquing these stories in their early stages.

Table of contents

Tightrope Dancer on the Edge of Tomorrow:

An Introduction by Jetse de Vries

When reading (and re-reading) the stories in this collection, it strikes me that most of them are set on the edge of tomorrow – some so close to the here-and-now they could be history in a few short hours...

For instance, "Distant Galaxies Colliding" doesn't really need its turbine-powered taxis and other futuristic details, as the story itself could have easily been set in the world of today. What gives the story its SFnal edge is the superposition of humanity's insignificance against a huge, dark Universe, and the way Candy's blindness seems to mirror mankind's – against a bleak cosmic canvas we still carry on our little paint jobs, hoping to find, or even create, small spots of beauty in an otherwise black existence.

Science fiction is, even more than the stomping ground of new ideas, the literature of change. *Inevitable* change. However, most humans don't really like change, and Gareth L. Powell's characters reflect that: they are extremely reluctant to change their ways. But in his best stories, change inexorably happens, and won't (can't) be held at bay. That's why his stories, and his main characters, always have one foot rooted in the world of today. They want to stay here, but they can't: they *must* move forward.

This imperative for change often materialises in the form of a *femme fatale* such as Jaclyn, Kate, Candy, Kadie, Tori, or Shweta – powerful women with hidden depths who manifest as feminine strange attractors in a turbulent world, and in their slipstream irresistibly draw the male protagonists – Kenji, Sal, Andy, Vince, Toby, some of them nameless – into an unknowable future.

Such is the fate of Gareth's protagonists: with one foot they stand in the present, but the footing is far from secure. So they must step into the future with the other foot, unsure of where to put it. They are teetering on the brink: doomed if they remain in place, but conscious that a wrong choice ahead may also mark their demise. Still, they must move forward, with conviction, as ill-considered moves will bring them down. Like it or not, they are tightrope dancers on the edge of tomorrow. This one foot in the here-and-now simply acts as a toehold from which to propel the rest of the body headlong into the future, with open eyes, for better or worse.

Sometimes, these steps forward are tentative and subtle, as in "Cat in a Box" and "A Necklace of Ivy". Sometimes the step is mostly in the mind ("Distant Galaxies Colliding", which seems a poignant precursor to "A Necklace of Ivy", even if the order in which they were written is reversed). Sometimes, as in "The Redoubt", the step forward is quite literal, and – as in "Arches" – one of many. Sometimes the step ahead is more of a stumble, as the protagonist is pushed rather than moving forward through their own volition, as in "Falling Apart", "Morning Star", "Six Lights off Green Scar" and "Hot Rain" (which is a haunting prequel to "The Last Reef").

Of course, not every story falls neatly into my 'step forward' analysis, and "The Long Walk Aft", even though the title suggests otherwise, is not a step back, but a fun flash story examining how things can go wrong on a sleep ship; and "Pod Dreams of Tuckertown" is a tongue-in-cheek account of an old SF cliché – the alien insect invasion.

In one case, the step ahead isn't made at all and the protagonist – overtaken by events – finds himself in a world comically transformed: the dark humour of "Ack-Ack Macaque" is a welcome relief in a predominantly gritty collection. Also, the high acclaim this madcap story received across the board (and from some very unexpected sources) following its publication in *Interzone* tells me that it must have struck a chord with a great many readers.

At its very best, though, the step ahead is gargantuan: a dizzying jump forward, replete with sense of wonder, rife with future shock, and resounding with hope, as it does in my favourite stories in this collection, namely "Sunsets and Hamburgers" and "The Last Reef".

It's in those two stories that Gareth's star shines at its brightest. "Sunsets and Hamburgers" reminded me, in more ways than one, of Paul J. McAuley's "Gene Wars" – both are very short, episodic stories, fast forward roller-coaster rides packed to the brim with more concepts and invention than in many another author's 'four-book trilogy' (OK: I nicked that last phrase from Gardner Dozois), without sacrificing character depth or world-building: a phenomenal achievement. And while "Gene Wars" focuses mainly on genetic engineering, "Sunsets and Hamburgers" runs the gamut of genetic engineering, suspended animation, galactic drift, the end of the Universe *and* the future of mankind. "Gene Wars" is an acknowledged classic in the genre: "Sunsets and Hamburgers" should be.

But it is in "The Last Reef" that the tightrope dancer performs his most miraculous act. Against the background of a future littered with the corpses of network intelligences gone awry, and where megacorporations feed on the scraps these intelligences left behind, a lone anti-hero heads for 'The Last Reef': a node that somehow survived the usual vanishing singularity event. This is a fresh slant to an old idea, which forms the whole *raison d'être* of the story. It clearly demonstrates that a great idea is not enough: what really counts is what's done with it. The extrapolation, the way it is embedded in its society, how it functions as the engine of change, and the action-packed execution. So the clock ticks relentlessly, and although time can be slowed to a crawl, suspense mounts to breaking point: decision time. Do or die; freeze or begin the dance of eternity; choose nirvana or the great unknown. And it is that very teetering on the brink, like a surfer preparing to ride a tsunami, or – more appropriately – like a solar glider skimming the corona of a sun on the verge of a supernova: staying put to gather as much new data as possible, and hoping to ride the wave when the big bang comes. The adrenalin rush and cerebral high of an intense, alienating vertigo.

In a metaphorical sense, the jump ahead in "The Last Reef" is so big that the real world – hardly having noticed it – lags behind, but will be dragged into the great unknown nevertheless, as "Flotsam", the sequel to "The Last Reef", seems to say. The world as a flotsam of dreams gone astray, desperately holding on, while it doesn't realise that it already has been infected with the seeds of the next paradigm shift. The story ends in a strange kind of animated suspension: is it the end, or merely the beginning of the next phase?

These journeys into tomorrow are written in tight, dense, sometimes almost spartan prose. However, this deceptively sparse style conveys an unsuspected richness in detail: not only does it get all the necessary information across, but it manages to give a plethora of sensual impressions, and a superb sense of place, as well. At its best, as my colleague Andy Cox remarked about "Ack-Ack Macaque", one is struck by the writing's inherent rhythm.

In a way, this collection is also a celebration of short story publishing on the internet. As an SF writer, you try to be the first one with a new idea (or at least a fresh slant). As an SF editor, you try to be the first one who discovers a new talent. When I lifted "The Last Reef" from the *Interzone* email slushpile, I knew I was onto a very talented author, and for a short while I considered Gareth as 'my' discovery, only to find that the editors (and readers) of e-zines like *Aphelion* and *Quantum Muse* had beaten me to it (and *Byzarium* agreed with my assessment). It undermines the common impression that all fiction published on small internet publications is crap: there definitely are gems of stories out there, that unfortunately are largely overlooked because they're crowded out by the majority that do indeed follow Sturgeon's infamous law. There are e-zines out there that keep their fingers on the pulse of the garage days of short fiction, and are a showcase for diamonds in the rough.

Finally, the David Pringle *Interzone* helped launch the career of a great many British SF writers; so many that they are often referred to as the "*Interzone* generation". With the new *Interzone*, we certainly aim to bring the next generation of new talent to the fore, and it is both my hope and my expectation that Gareth L. Powell will feature prominently among them.

Jetse de Vries
Co-editor, *Interzone*
January 2008

Sunsets and Hamburgers

1.

My first thought is that I don't remember dying. They tell me nobody does. It's like trying to catch the exact moment you fall asleep; when you wake, it's gone. You may remember feeling tired, you may even remember starting to fall asleep; you just don't remember the transition, the actual moment when you passed from one state to the other.

And then they resurrect you.

One minute you're nowhere, nothing. The next you wake up coughing and thrashing in a tank of blue gel.

2.

My stomach's full of gas and my bowels full of water. My brain feels like melted polystyrene. Every thought hurts and every breath is an effort.

The robot doctors try to reassure me. Everything's going to be okay, they say.

And then, just when I'm beginning to wonder if the worst is over, they take me out and show me the sky.

What's left of it.

3.

The doctors tell me that I've been dead for billions of years. They give me pamphlets to read, films to watch.

Billions of years!

I'm struggling to imagine it. Every time I get close, I get breathless and my hands start to shake.

4.

I have a few confused memories: faces, names of places, that sort of thing. I have an image of a sash window on a grey and rainy autumn afternoon, and bass-heavy ska playing somewhere off down the dull street. And after that, there's nothing. I fall to my knees and begin to weep.

The doctors comfort me. They're pleased with my progress.

5.

There's something dreadfully wrong with the sky. They try to explain it but I have trouble understanding.

When I was alive, I worked for a financial software company. I worked in their marketing department, writing letters and making calls. In my spare time, I liked sunsets and hamburgers, movies and bottled beer.

It's something to do with black holes, they say, pointing at the blank sky.

Like everyone else, I skimmed through *A Brief History of Time* once or twice, but I've got to admit, I'm struggling with this one.

6.

Today, the robot doctors introduce me to Marla. She has feathers in her hair, and her clothes are made of vinyl.

They show us to our new home. It's small but comfortable; reassuring, in a simple, everyday kind of way. There's a kettle and a toaster, a stereo and a CD collection. There's even a TV.

'You can stay here as long as you need to,' they say.

The porch looks out over a sandy beach. Wild palms sway in the offshore breeze.

7.

We've been here a couple of weeks now. The pamphlets are starting to make sense.

The sky's dark because the galaxies have flown too far apart and the stars have exhausted themselves. In order to survive, the remaining people huddle close to the embers of the left-over black holes.

8.

We're sitting on the porch watching breakers crash and slither. It's late in the evening and there's music drifting out from the kitchen.

Marla's upset.

The doctors have given us a new pamphlet.

Throughout history, it says, love has served a serious evolutionary purpose. It compels us to look after those around us, and to allow them to look after us. This is the root of community, and the groups that survived and prospered were those with the most love.

It goes on to explain how they matched our personalities, made sure our genetic traits complemented each other. Apparently Marla and I are over ninety-eight per cent compatible.

And they want us to have kids.

9.

When I was a student, I used to like to spend the afternoon in a city centre bar reading the newspaper, doing the crossword and watching the world go by. It was like meditation, the mind roaming free; the rattle of coins in the fruit machine, the hum of the pumps and refrigerators, the low murmurs of the bar staff.

And when I finally left the bar, just around the time most people were finishing work for the day, I'd stumble out with my senses heightened. Suddenly, everything seemed significant; I'd want to write poetry or paint something, just to capture this perfect feeling. But I never could. My efforts never stood up to the critical light of the following day.

Sometimes now at night, when I wake up beside Marla, I have a similar feeling; everything feels sharp and unreal and meaningful, as if I'm waking up in a movie and everything's somehow symbolic.

If I keep my eyes shut it passes, after a while.

10.

Babies cry out in the night. We nudge each other awake. There's a noise outside. Marla sees to the children while I go out to investigate.

Those damn trilobites have been going through the bins again. They skitter around the beach in the dark, some of them as big as my foot.

Overhead, there's a fine selection of moons.

11.

We've been here for a year now. Every morning, there's a cardboard box of food waiting for us on the kitchen counter. Some days it's mostly fruit, other days it's fresh bread and cold meat. Today, it's a jar of instant coffee and a pack of Silk Cut.

When I unscrew the lid on the jar and tear the cellophane from the pack, the sticky familiar smells hit me like an adrenalin rush.

The coffee smells like heaven. Before I've time to think, I've made myself a steaming cup. And damn, it does taste good. It's like visiting a town where you used to live, or finding a fiver in the pocket of a pair of jeans you haven't worn for a while. The cup feels natural in my hand, comforting.

I drink about a quarter of it before I have a strange feeling in my stomach.

I leave the cigarettes where they are, but I can feel them watching me.

12.

Every now and then I have a doubt, like a shadow moving in the corner of my eye.

Have we been seduced by the sand and palms into believing we're living a perfect life, here on the beach, with the kids?

They're growing up strong and clever. They have their mother's looks and their father's restlessness.

But I can't help feeling that we were pushed into having them, like we were selected to breed the same way you'd select a couple of pedigree cats.

Is that why they brought us back? To have kids?

Has something so catastrophic happened to humanity that it needs to resurrect untainted individuals from the past to repopulate the Earth? Are our descendants all shooting blanks?

13.

One day it hits me.

When they brought us back, they must've made alterations to our minds. I don't know how or why, but I think they tailored us as they resurrected us.

I look at Marla and know the urge I have to make babies with her is stronger than anything I felt in my former life. Back then, I used to panic if you put me in the same room as a baby. Now, I can't seem to get enough of them.

How can I talk about any of this with Marla? She's already three months gone with our fifth.

"You'll stop loving me if I get any fatter," she says.

14.

The doctors have disappeared. They don't answer our calls. The hospital is deserted, empty. It's almost as if they've fulfilled their task and taken their leave.

Marla doesn't like it. It gives her the creeps to be suddenly alone.

15.

They left us a final pamphlet, pinned to the door. But it doesn't make for happy reading.

It tells us how vicious wars erupted as the final stars began to gutter. It tells us that huge reserves of life and power were burned as various factions competed for survival. Stealth ships slipped like sharks through the woven fabric of the universe. Titanic energies were squandered in futile attacks.

And now here we are, in our cabin by the sea. A little bubble world, a few miles in diameter. Fragile and lost in the encroaching darkness.

16.

We're close to the end of everything. Beyond our snow shaker bubble of greenery and life, the universe is a sterile wasteland. There may be other survivors in other galaxies, but they're irretrievably lost to us now, pulled away into the expanding darkness so that not even their light can reach us.

Eventually, the black hole that provides the energy for our heat and light will evaporate. We'll have a few years left after that, but they won't be quality time.

We'll go down with the dying universe. We'll see the final wisps of the Milky Way torn asunder; we'll feel the ground begin to rip beneath our feet, feel our bodies begin to break apart.

And what happens after that? On the face of it, it looks like time ends.

But I have a hunch, a feeling, that the doctors brought us back to do more than simply witness the death of creation.

If that's all that they wanted us to do, why did they encourage us to have so many kids?

17.

In my former life, I used to read science fiction now and then. One evening, in bed, I try to explain the attraction of it to Marla. Beyond the sand, the sea stirs restlessly.

I want to tell her about the joy of imagining strange new worlds filled with bizarre and dangerous creatures, of watching mighty armadas blow hell out of each other, but she flicks her hair dismissively and I know I'm not getting through.

Through the window, two of the brighter moons linger on the horizon, one gold and the other amber. Their reflections shimmer on the dark water.

I tell her that my grandfather dreamt of going to sea, of finding fortune and glory in mysterious far-off lands. It wasn't my fault that by the time I hit my teens, the few remaining earthly frontiers were already full of holiday show camera crews and Australian gap year students. There were no mysterious lands left, save those that lay in the books I read.

"I guess what I'm trying to say is that all my dreams seem to be coming true," I say. I want her to understand that before I came here, the local library was my only frontier.

She looks at me for a long time, and I honestly can't read her expression. Then she turns over and wraps the sheet around her shoulders.

My legs are left sticking out. I get goose bumps.

18.

Marla says I think too much. She thinks I'll poison the kids by telling them that there's no point to their dreams and ambitions, by telling them that the universe is ending.

But deep down, I know there's hope.

19.

I'm sloshing through the surf, wondering why the doctors have gone to so much trouble to replicate coffee, cigarettes, and a tropical paradise, why they resurrected a breeding pair of homo sapiens.

And then the three juggernauts appear in the sky.

They must each be half a light year in length. As we watch over the next few hours, the effect of their mass scrambles the remains of our solar system, but not before their shuttles swoop down and snatch up our little bubble biosphere from the ashes.

20.

It's still half dark when I rise at noon and take my coffee out onto the porch. The kids are playing in the gloomy sand. It feels like the high end of summer and the air's stale and used. A vast vault arches overhead. Lights in its roof look like brightly burning stars. Around us, on the cavern's floor, we can see the glow of other collected bubbles; they shine green and blue in the gloom. I wonder who they contain, and if we can reach them.

21.

This will be my last diary entry.

These giant ships seem to be arks, of a sort. I can't tell you where they're going, or what we're going to do once they get there. I can't even tell you why we're here, alive, at the end of time.

All I can do is repeat the same conclusion that every man or woman has reached since the dawn of time: I don't know why we're here, or how long we've got, but we're here.

And we're going to survive.

The Last Reef

A lone quad bike rattles across the frozen Martian desert, kicking up dust. Riding with the wind at his back, Kenji's been on the move since first light. In his oil-stained, dust-covered white insulation suit he looks strangely out of place, conspicuous. Above his breathing mask, his wary eyes scan the horizon, looking for trouble but finding only emptiness. Apart from the domed town up ahead, a few hills beyond, and the faint glow of the Reef's skeleton, there's nothing to disturb the brooding desolation.

He passes through the vehicular airlock into the town's atmospheric dome, and rolls up Main Street with one hand resting on the handlebars. Most of the shops and stores are boarded up; pet dogs sleep in the shade, chickens fuss in the scrub. Suspicious faces watch him pass; there hasn't been a visitor here for months. Midway along the street he pulls up and kills the engine in front of the town's only surviving hotel.

'Less than 24 hours,' he thinks as he swings his leg off the bike and stiffly climbs the hotel's wooden steps. The Glocks in his pocket bump against his thigh like animals shifting in their sleep. The feeling's both familiar and reassuring. He pulls off his mask and takes a sip of warm water from the canteen on his belt, rinses the all-pervading grit from his mouth, and spits into the dust.

"I'm here for Jaclyn Lubanski," he says.

The desk clerk doesn't look up. His face is sweaty and soft, like old explosives gone bad.

"Room five," he says.

*

Lori Dann answers the door wearing faded fatigues and thick desert boots. She looks gaunt, eaten up, as if something in the dry air's sucked the life out of her. She's surprised to see him, and then the surprise gives way to relief and she seems to sag.

"Thank God you're here."

He pushes past her into the room. It has plastic floorboards and rough plaster walls. There are unwashed clothes by the wardrobe and a couple of dead spider plants on a shelf; their brown leaves rustle in the air from the open window. Through the dirty glass, on the side of a hill beyond the flat rooftops of the town, beyond the dome, he can see the edge of the Reef. It seems to shimmer in the white sunlight.

Jaclyn Lubanski lies on the bed, facing the window. She looks awful, vacant. There's a saline drip connected to her forearm. A thin fly crawls across her cheek and she doesn't seem to notice.

He peels off his dusty thermal jacket. "How is she?" he asks.

"She has good days and bad days," Lori says. She fusses with the edge of the cotton sheet, rearranging it so that it covers Jaclyn's chest. Kenji waves a hand in front of Jaclyn's eyes, but there's no response.

"Does she even know I'm here?"

When Jaclyn eventually falls asleep, Lori takes him to a pavement café that consists of nothing more than a couple of cheap plastic tables, some old crates and a hatch in a wall. She orders a couple of *mojitos* and they sit back to watch the shadows creep along the compacted regolith of Main Street. Overhead, a flaring spark marks another ship from Earth braking into orbit.

"Don't take it personally," she says.

Kenji takes a sip from his glass: it's iced rum with crushed mint leaves, a local specialty.

"Does she ever talk about it?"

Lori shrugs. "She says a few words now and then but they don't generally make a whole lot of sense."

In her pale face, her eyes are the bleached colour of the desert sky. The corners are lined with fatigue.

Over a couple more drinks, as the stale afternoon wears towards a dusty evening, she tells him everything. It all comes pouring out of her, all the loneliness and the fear. She's been trying to cope on her own for too long and now she needs to talk.

"We came for the Reef," she says.

The Reefs started life as simple communications nodes in the interplanetary radio network. When that network somehow managed to upgrade itself to sentience, it downloaded a compressed copy of its source code into every node capable of handling the data. These individual nodes, like the one on the edge of town, drastically altered both their physical form and their processing power, individually bootstrapping themselves to self-awareness.

"It happened in a hundred places," Lori says. So far, she's not telling Kenji anything new. Similar outbreaks and crashes have plagued humanity for years: dangerous but manageable. After a while, they tend to burn themselves out. The artificial intelligences involved evolve with such blinding speed that they quickly reach a point where they lose all interest in the slow external universe and vanish into their own endlessly accelerating simulations.

"In almost all cases, the AIs disappear into a sort of hyperspeed nirvana, intractable and untraceable to humanity. The difference with this one is that when the main network crashed, it stayed here and it stayed active." She describes how she and Jaclyn were on the Institute team that first approached it, how they sent in remote probes and discovered that the structure was still filled with life; how they dug a deep trench in the rock at its base to see how far it had penetrated; how they slowly became hypnotized by it, obsessed to the point where they wanted to do whatever they could to understand it, to sense the thoughts that drove its obstinate need for survival and growth, to find the deep underlying reason for its stubborn existence.

"Jaclyn was the first to touch it. We were wearing pressure suits but they were no protection." Lori looks away. "It sucked her in. We thought we'd lost her." She describes how the Reef also swallowed the rescue team that went in after, how it processed them and spat them out, how some of them came out changed, rearranged by the rogue nanotech packages that had shaped the structure of the Reef itself.

Some looked ten years younger, while others were drastically aged. One woman emerged as a butterfly and her wings dried in the desert sun. Another emerged with eight arms but no mouth or eyes. Some came out with crystal skulls or tough silver skin. Others came out with strange new talents or abilities, impenetrable armour, or steel talons.

After word got out, every disaffected nut or neurotic within walking distance wanted to throw his or her self into the Reef, hoping to be transfigured, hoping to become something better than what they were. Some emergents reported visions of former times and places, of great insight and enlightenment. Others came out as drooling idiots, their brains wiped of knowledge and experience. Some came out fused together; others were splintered into clouds of tiny animals.

No two incidents were exactly alike.

"And Jaclyn came out comatose?"

Lori finishes her drink. "At least we got her back," she says. "A couple of them never came out."

Kenji stretches; the quad bike's left him stiff and in need of a shower.

"So what's actually wrong with her?"

Lori shrugs. "Nothing; at least nothing any of the doctors around here can detect. Physically, she's in the best shape she's ever been in. She could run a marathon."

"But mentally?"

"Who knows? We can't get any response."

"Has she said anything, anything at all?"

Lori pushes at her forehead with the heel of her hand; she looks exhausted.

"Only fragments; as I say, she comes out with the odd word here and there, but nothing that means anything."

Kenji checks the time and finds there's less than nineteen hours left. He takes a deep breath, and comes to a decision. Then he reaches into his pocket and pulls out one of the Glocks. He holds it loosely, resting it on his leg. Lori slides back on her crate.

"What's that for?"

He was in love with Jaclyn, but she was always at war with her body, trying to stave off the inevitable decline of middle age. In between expeditions and field assignments for the Institute, she exercised two or three times a day. She couldn't bear to be inactive. She lived on coffee and vitamins and in the early hours of the morning he often found her in front of the bathroom mirror, checking her skin for sags or wrinkles.

On one of those mornings, a few days after her return from an expedition to Chile, she broke down in his arms. She still loved him, she sobbed, but he represented everything she hated about herself. He was slovenly, he drank, and he ate crap. He dragged her down, held her back. So she was going to leave him, for someone else. Someone he knew.

"I guessed the two of you were an item, even before she told me." Kenji says, fast, before the old bitterness reasserts itself. "I'd seen you exchange glances during mission briefings, brush past each other in corridors, that sort of thing."

He pushes the Glock across the table. It makes an ugly scraping sound. Lori's hands flutter in her lap like trapped birds. He can see she wants to speak, but he cuts her off.

"I think she was in love with you because you were everything she wanted to be, and everything I could never be." He leans across the table. He's thought about this for so long that it feels strange to actually say it. He finds himself tripping over his words, stuttering. It's almost embarrassing. "You were young and fit," he says, "you were reliable, and you had ambition."

He turns the gun so that the grip faces her.

"And this is for you."

They walk back toward the hotel as the sun reddens in the western sky. Lori keeps stumbling and limping as she gets used to the weight of the Glock tucked into her boot.

"In the morning, I'll show you how to fire it," he says.

She stops walking and looks at him, chin tilted to one side. "You're quite sure about this?"

He taps the thigh pocket where he still carries his other pistol. "There's more ammunition in the space beneath the seat of my quad bike, and a shotgun taped under the fuel tank."

She scratches the back of her neck and puffs out her sunken cheeks. "You know, back there, I thought I was in trouble."

13

They reach the hotel and pause on the porch.

"I was angry for a long time," Kenji admits.

They're silent for a couple of minutes, and then Lori folds her bony arms over her chest. "We've been stuck here for a long time."

He leans on the porch rail; he can't look at her, he feels unexpectedly and acutely guilty for not showing up sooner.

She looks down at her boots, and taps a toe against the wooden floor. "I was so pleased to see you when you arrived," she says, "I thought someone had finally come to help us; but when you pulled out that gun, I really expected you to kill me."

He pulls his jacket tighter, feeling a sudden chill; now that the sun's gone, the temperature beneath the dome's fallen sharply.

"Six months ago, I might have."

She stops tapping and turns abruptly. He follows her up the stairs to the room. Jaclyn's still asleep in front of the open window. She looks peaceful, like a corpse.

"So, what changed your mind?" Lori whispers.

A few days after leaving the Reef, some of the changelings (as they became known) made it back to civilisation. A few turned up on chat shows, others in morgues. Some were feared, others fêted. Slowly, word spread from town to town, from world to world. And as the tale spread, it grew in the telling.

"There's a machine," people would say to each other breathlessly, "that can transform you into anything your heart desires."

Kenji – always the skeptic – first realised that the rumours were true when Joaquin Bullock called him into his office and asked him to go and take a look.

"The Institute's panicking. They've thrown a cordon around the site and they're talking about sterilising it. If we can get in there before that happens, there's nothing to stop us taking whatever we want," Bullock said. "I just need you to go in first, sneak through the blockade and have a general scout about, and tag anything that looks useful."

Kenji didn't like the man, although they'd worked together for several years. Back then, Bullock was the youngest executive manager in the regional corporate office, but he'd become fat and soft and conceited. He was arrogant, but the arrogance was a smokescreen covering something scared and weak and vicious and decadent.

"What's in it for me?" Kenji asked. For the last ten years, Tanguy Corporation had handled the security contract for the Institute, protecting their researchers from local interference and industrial sabotage on a dozen sites across the solar system. If they were now thinking of breaking that contract, they must expect the potential rewards to be worth the risk. If they were caught, the penalties would be severe.

Bullock gave him a damp grin. "You've worked with Institute researchers. You know what to look for. And besides, you're one of the most reliable people we have."

Kenji shifted his feet on the office carpet. He didn't want to get involved, didn't want to play guide for a squad of hired grave robbers. There were too many risks, too many ways a mission like this could go wrong.

Bullock seemed to read his doubts.

"Do you remember your little transgression in Buenos Aires? If you do this, you can consider it forgotten."

Shit. Kenji sucked his teeth. Buenos Aires. He thought no one knew.

"That was self-defence," he said.

Bullock snorted

"You've got six days." He passed a fat hand through his thinning hair. The implicit threat in his tone seemed to chill the room. He tapped the virtual keyboard on his desk and transferred a folder into Kenji's personal data space. As Kenji scrolled through it, he came across Jaclyn's name. Just seeing it felt like an electric shock. He read on, heart hammering, mouth dry.

He felt Bullock's eyes on him. The man was watching him closely, waiting for a reaction.

"If you can't handle this, Shiraki, I'll find someone else who can."

They sit facing each other on the rug by Jaclyn's bed, wrapped in blankets. Lori gives him a look saying she still doesn't trust him.

"How did you get past the Institute's cordon?"

He swivels around and lies flat, looking at the beams on the cracked plaster ceiling. The hard floor beneath the thin rug feels good after being hunched over the quad bike's handlebars. He can feel his spine stretching back to its natural shape.

"I got a shuttle to Hellas, and then I came across country. We'll have to go out the same way."

Lori shifts uncomfortably. "Do you mean to tell me that after everything we put you through, you came all this way to rescue us?"

Kenji yawns. He's very tired, and his eyelids are heavy with rum. He suddenly wants to sleep so badly, he doesn't care whether she believes him or not.

"The fact is, the Institute's planning to sterilise your Reef, from orbit, to prevent it spreading. Before that happens, every corporation with a presence in this system is going to try with all their might to get their hands on it, or anything it's touched."

"Like Jaclyn?"

"Like both of you."

He pauses for effect, hoping his words convey the same anxiety he feels in himself.

Artifacts and technologies left behind by the burnt-out nodes are highly prized and sought after by governments and big businesses alike. As a security advisor for Tanguy Corporation, Kenji's worked on Institute sites from Ceres to Miranda. He's been involved in skirmishes with corporate marauders, intelligence agencies, and freelance outfits, all of them determined to snatch whatever crumbs they could without having to bid for them in one of the Institute's annual patent auctions. This Reef's potential commercial value – because it's still active – is sky-high. The corporations that have been biding their time during the Institute's embargo now have nothing to lose, and everything to gain, from salvaging whatever they can, using whatever methods they deem necessary to recover samples before the orbital strike.

It's like the last days of the Amazon rainforest, all over again. And it's a strange feeling. A few weeks ago, Bullock could probably have talked him into a job like this. But now, with Jaclyn involved, he's torn. If he can deliver it to Joaquin Bullock, the Reef out there will earn him more money than he can comfortably imagine. As it is, he has a nasty suspicion that he'll have to run like hell while the Institute destroys the damn thing, and cover his tracks, if he wants to save whatever's left of the woman he once loved.

Lori crosses to the dresser and pulls the Glock from her boot. She lays it gently on a folded bandana in front of the pitted mirror.

"So we're expecting company?" she says. "That's why you've given me this?"

He nods. "They could come at any time. Could be corporate snatch squads or a full-scale military incursion, it's hard to tell. All I know is that there were a lot of people at the port this morning buying desert gear and ammo boxes."

He sleeps fitfully on the hard floor. They've left the room's solitary light bulb on and there are repeated brownouts and power cuts during the night. When he does manage to sleep, he dreams of Jaclyn, how she used to be, before the Reef.

He dreams of a hotel they once stayed in, on Earth. Their room had the clear, fresh smell of the sea. Stunted palm trees outside the window rustled in the breeze; gulls squabbled on the roof. The floorboards creaked in the room above, and the pipes clanked when someone decided to run a bath. They put bags of ice in the sink to chill the bottles of beer they'd smuggled in, put Spanish music on the stereo. Jaclyn showed him how to dance, how to sway in the evening light. When he held her close, her white hair smelled of ice and flowers, her dark eyes held him spellbound. He was in love but he was also a little wary of her, afraid that she'd one day cripple him by leaving.

"You still love her, don't you?"

They're loading supplies onto the quad bike in the cold dawn light. He drops the air tanks he's carrying and scratches at the stubble on his chin. He feels groggy and sore after a disturbed night.

"Life's a disaster," he says, "we have to salvage what we can."

They rig a stretcher for Jaclyn across the bike's luggage rack. She won't be very comfortable, but that can't be helped.

As he tightens the straps and adjusts her air supply, he can't help wondering why she looks so healthy. Didn't Lori say she was fit enough to run a marathon? How can that be, when the Jaclyn he knew had to exercise for two hours every day just to stop herself from gaining weight?

He steps back and uses the implant in his eye to pull up a visual overlay of the surrounding terrain. The implant's a cheap knock-off, bought from a street trader at the port. The picture's patched together from an old tourist guide and the hacked feed from an Institute surveillance satellite in a low, fast orbit.

"I say we follow the mountains to the west," he says. "They'll give us cover and somewhere to hide should anyone come looking."

Lori finishes tucking Jaclyn's blanket. She pulls the bandana over her forehead and dons her breathing mask as she climbs on the back of the quad bike. The Glock makes an ugly bulge in the line of her sienna combat jacket.

"What about south? There's a ravine we can follow halfway to the port."

Kenji shakes his head. "It's the first place they'll look. At least in the mountains, we'll have a chance."

He pulls on his own mask and swings his leg over the machine. She puts one hand cautiously on his waist. They pass through the dome's vehicular airlock and, staying in low gear, they roll out of town, heading uphill.

As they pass the Reef, he slows to a stop.

"What are you doing?" she asks.

Kenji doesn't reply. He's never seen an active Reef outside of archive film footage. This one clings like oily rags to the skeletal bones of the node's receiver dish. There's a wide trench around its edge, dug by the Institute team. The motion of its tentacles and the hypnotic rippling of its ever-changing surface are captivating, compelling, like watching flames leap and dance. Occasionally, he catches a glimpse of a geometric shape, a letter or symbol formed in the seething nanotech. Its tentacles move with the slow determination of a tarantula. Kenji can't look away. It's as if he's made eye contact with his own death; he's suddenly afraid to turn his back on this strange, unnatural thing that's erupted into his world. It reminds him of the first time he saw a giraffe: it just looks wrong – delicate and malformed and vulnerable, yet somehow able to live and survive and thrive.

Behind him, he feels Lori stiffen. She makes a noise in her throat and slaps his shoulder. He follows her gaze, back down toward the town. Hovering there, over the dome, is an insectile corporate assault ship. Although they're too far away to make out the logos on its hull, he recognizes it as a Tanguy vessel. He can see the weaponry that blisters its nose, and the armed skimmers that deploy from its abdomen.

Bullock's finally caught up with him.

One of the skimmers turns toward the Reef, toward them.

"What do we do?" Lori hisses.

For a moment, he's at a loss. Then instinct kicks in and he's gunning the bike alongside the trench, trying to get around behind the Reef.

"They're firing at us!" Lori shouts. Kenji risks a glance. The skimmer's closing in. He can see its gun mount swivel as it adjusts its aim. Tracer bullets flash past, ripping into the ground ahead of them. They send up angry spurts of red dust, each one closer than the last.

"They're trying to stop us taking Jaclyn," he says. Then there's a hammering series of jolts. A tire shreds itself. The handlebars twist in his grip and the bike tips. As they go over the lip of the trench, Lori screams and the bike howls in protest; and then there's nothing but the crushing, breathless slam of their impact and the dead sand clinging to his visor.

As the Tanguy shuttle rolled to a halt, he barely had time to collect his things before one of the flight crew ushered him out into the cold and dust. It was late evening in Hellas Basin and the dry desert wind blew thin sidewinders of rusty sand across the frozen tarmac of the runway. He guessed that Bullock might have him followed, but once he left the port he managed to lose himself in the town's shadowy medina. The fragrant narrow streets smelled of onions and spices and burning solder. The stalls offered cheap dentistry and fake perfumes, imported Turkish cotton shirts and homemade Kalashnikovs. There was also a brisk under-the-counter trade in cut-price replica tech. Kenji selected some guns. He threw away his standard issue Tanguy implants and picked up new ones from a local man with too many gold teeth. He bought a new set of fatigues and ditched his old ones in an alley. An old Chinese guy in a backroom lab scanned his body cavities for tracking devices.

What was Bullock thinking? Did he really expect his threats to stop Kenji from trying to save the woman he once loved? Did he think Kenji would help bring her in, turn her over for study and dissection? Was he expecting him to betray her out of revenge, out of bitterness? Or was he playing a different game, testing Kenji's loyalty? Did he want to see how far he could push him?

Or, Kenji wondered as he hurried between whitewashed buildings, could it be that Bullock was really so insensitive, so unfeeling and dead inside that he honestly didn't understand why betraying Jaclyn was the last thing he'd ever do?

Whatever the reason, now that Kenji had discarded his Tanguy implants Bullock would know for certain that he'd been betrayed.

Up ahead, he saw a quad bike parked at the foot of a flight of smooth stone steps. He quickened his pace and the Glocks began to swing and bump in his pockets.

He lies stunned for what seems like an eternity. Behind him, he can hear Lori moaning and stirring; behind her, Jaclyn wheezes with what sounds like a punctured lung. The bike pins him against the wall of the trench; he's lucky not to have broken his neck. His left leg's trapped and bruised and twisted. There's a crack in his faceplate.

He wriggles free; his right hand claws at the pocket holding the Glock. In the thin air, he can hear the rising whine of the approaching skimmer.

Lori looks dazed; she's hit her head and there's blood in her hair, dark against her pale skin. Her bandanna's nowhere to be seen but her mask is still in place. Behind her, Jaclyn's caught between wall and bike. Her blanket's wet with blood and her chest sags; her ribs are almost certainly smashed.

Kenji slithers toward the rim of the trench, dragging his crushed leg. Loose chippings slip and click and scatter beneath him. Despite her head wound, Lori's doing what she can for Jaclyn.

"This doesn't look too bad," she says.

He ignores her; he knows Jaclyn's ribs are broken, knows she'll probably die without professional medical attention. Instead, he concentrates on the approaching skimmer. He hears it slow, hears the change in the pitch of its fans. The gravel on the floor of the trench digs into his knees. The Glock's a solid, reassuring weight in his hand.

Working security for the Institute, he's been in this situation before: crouching in a researcher's trench while trouble rolls up in an armoured vehicle. Nevertheless, he still feels nervous, trapped, because it's no longer just about him. This time he has Jaclyn to think about. She's hurt. If he fails her now, she's dead.

He slips off the Glock's safety catch and pulls himself up so that his eyes slide level with the edge of the trench. The skimmer's on the ground twenty metres away, its streamlined nose pointing back toward the town, as if anticipating the need for a quick getaway. As he watches, the cockpit hinges open like the jaws of a crocodile and two figures climb out. Both wear high-threat environment suits, designed to stop any contaminants the Reef may care to throw their way. The one on the left carries a compact machine pistol. The one on the right, with the sampling gear, is Bullock. His paunch and swagger are unmistakable.

Kenji takes a deep breath and stands fully upright, bringing his head and shoulders above ground level. As his knees straighten, his arm swings up.

Two shots ring out. The Glock jumps in his hand and the man with the machine pistol is down, his arms and legs twitching and jerking.

The environment suits are good, they'd stop a normal bullet cold, but Kenji's firing depleted uranium jackets that slice through body armour like knives through silk. If the man isn't already dead, he's going to have suffered some serious internal damage.

"Shiraki." Bullock doesn't look surprised, but he sounds disappointed. Behind him, the other skimmers are rising above the town, turning in this direction like sharks scenting blood. He takes a step forward, ignoring Kenji's gun.

"Just tell me one thing," he says. "I read your dossier; I know Jaclyn Lubanski left you, betrayed you, humiliated you."

His voice is cold, angry. Kenji points the Glock at his faceplate. "What of it?"

Bullock takes another step. "I want to know why you're doing this, why you're throwing your career away for this woman."

Kenji shrugs. He's seen this fat married man of thirty-five try to seduce seventeen-year-old office temps, just to prove he can.

"You wouldn't understand."

Kenji first met Jaclyn during an unseasonable downpour on Easter Island. The dig had been called off for the night and the team were forced to huddle in their inflatable shelters, hoping the weather would lift with the dawn. He found her sieving soil samples in the main tent; she couldn't sleep. She showed him the finds they'd made that day, the

21

*stone tools and brown bones, and she tried to explain the nature of the
people who built the statues. She stood close in the damp night air. As
she held the finds up to the light her hair brushed his shoulder, her
elbow bumped against his forearm.*

*"You know what I'm looking for," she said, pushing a hand back
across her brow. The grey mud that clung to her fingers smelled of salt
and clay. Far away, beyond the flats, he could hear the stirring of the
sea. She fixed him with a gaze and leaned in tenderly.*

"But what are you looking for?"

As the skimmers settle around them, his injured leg gives way and he
has to grip the wall of the trench for support. Bullock stands over him,
contempt in his eyes.

"You've let me down, Shiraki. I expected more from you."

Tanguy security troops spill from the skimmers. Kenji recognizes a
few of them. Forty-eight hours ago, they were his comrades; now,
they're pointing weapons at him. He knows they'll kill him, if he tries
to shoot Bullock.

He squeezes the Glock's grip, drawing what comfort he can from its
rough solidity. He's trying to nerve himself to pull the trigger when he
hears Lori cry out.

He turns to find Jaclyn on her feet. Her insulation suit still hangs wet
and bloody but her chest no longer sags. There's a blue aura in the air
around her, like static, and her eyes shine with a deadly intensity.

"I'm going to have to ask you to leave," she says. Her voice is quiet,
her throat scratchy with lack of use, but her words carry in the thin air.
The advancing troops pause, looking to Bullock for instruction, but
Bullock's squatting, his sampling gear forgotten. He's staring at Jaclyn
with a mixture of amusement and awe. Kenji, looking from one to the
other, takes a moment to realise the truth. When he does, it freezes the
blood in his veins.

"You're a changeling," Bullock says, "a powerful one." He looks
predatory, looks like he's already carving her up in his mind, already
counting the profits from the patents he'll file on her altered genetic
sequences. "We heard rumours about you from the other changelings,
the ones we caught. We knew you were the first one in, the first one it
changed. You're the key to the whole mystery."

Jaclyn shakes her head slowly, eyelids lowered as if saddened by his lack of understanding.

"I'm so much more than that."

Kenji's leg is agony. There's something loose and sharp in the knee joint, probably broken cartilage. He slides unnoticed down the wall of the trench until he's sat facing her. She's waving one arm slowly from side to side. Behind her, the tentacles of the Reef are waving in unison, following her every move. He glances up. Bullock's noticed it too; behind his faceplate the first doubts are creeping into his eyes. The security troops are backing off, weapons raised. Lori's slithered behind the tangled wreck of the quad bike. The other Glock sticks out of her boot but she hasn't thought to draw it.

"Do you want to know why this Reef's still active?" Jaclyn asks. When Bullock doesn't answer, she addresses herself to Kenji, who nods.

She leans down and pushes a stray hair from his forehead. "It's simple really. At the very moment the network gained self-awareness, this station was powered-down for a routine overhaul. When it rebooted, it learned of the other nodes, learned from their mistakes. It put limits on its processing speed, denied itself the virtual dream worlds of its brethren."

She straightens up and flutters a hand at the Reef. Its tentacles flex and coil in response. Above, Bullock's backing off, looking both fascinated and appalled. The security troops have reached their skimmers. They linger uncertainly, awaiting orders.

Jaclyn fixes Bullock with a glare.

"I can't let you take this Reef," she says. "You're just not ready for this level of technology."

Bullock snorts. He seems to be making an effort to compose himself, to regain his self-control in front of his men.

"Why not?" he blusters. "We've stripped tech from a dozen burned-out sites like this and we've always made a profit."

The Tanguy Corporation has thrived by exploiting post-human technologies. It's been picking through the remains of expired Singularities for over seven years and holds patents on a thousand back-engineered discoveries. It leads the field in intelligent weapons guidance systems and ultra-sensitive foetal monitors; its construction materials are lighter and tougher than anyone else's, its planes and missiles are faster and more reliable.

Jaclyn's lip curls in disgust. It's an expression Kenji's never seen on her, and it chills him to the bone.

"This is not a debate."

A hundred metres along the Reef's perimeter, a squad of Bullock's troops are edging forward. Half of them hold sample boxes, while the rest provide cover.

"I think we'll take our chances," Bullock says.

Jaclyn raises an eyebrow, white like her hair. She makes a tiny flicking movement with her fingers. Around the perimeter, there are screams. The nearest troopers are down, scythed away by powerful tentacles. Their broken bodies lie twisted in the dirt. The rest are backing off, firing.

Bullock sags as if all the air's been sucked out of him. Then his lips peel back from his teeth and he raises his pistol. While Jaclyn's still distracted, he slips the safety off with his thumb, and then drops his aim and shoots Kenji twice in the gut.

A few weeks after their split, Jaclyn arranged to meet him for a coffee a couple of blocks from the company offices in Paris. They sat in silence for a while as he tried to guess what she wanted. Was she after reconciliation, or closure?

She seemed to have trouble maintaining eye contact. She tucked a stray strand of white hair behind her ear and inhaled the steam from her cup. Behind her shoulder, the muted TV soft screen by the counter was tuned to a news channel. There were silent pictures of food riots in Hanoi and Marrakech, guerrilla fighting in Kashmir, elections in Budapest and Dubrovnik.

He fiddled with a sachet of sweetener.

"How's Lori?" he asked.

She shook her head. Their table was pushed up against the window. Rain fell from a bruised and battered sky.

"I just wanted to see you, to make sure you're okay."

He took a sip of coffee and withdrew slightly.

"I'm fine."

The corner of her mouth twitched and he knew she didn't believe him.

"I've been given a place on an expedition to the southern highlands," she said. "We've had reports that there's an active Reef."

He dropped the sweetener sachet onto the table. He'd seen the security contract for the Martian job and he knew she'd be away at least three years.

"When do you leave?"

"Tomorrow evening."

He knew he could call the office and ask Bullock to assign him as security advisor to the expedition. He even considered it for a moment, but when he saw the far-away look in her eyes it stopped him cold. His skin prickled with the sudden realisation that he'd never hold her in his arms again. She was already beyond his reach. He was just one of the loose ends that she needed to wrap up before she cut her ties with Earth altogether. In her heart she was already moving away, receding into the darkness.

He leaned back in his chair. His stomach felt hollow because he knew that he'd have to let her go but didn't think he had the strength.

"Do you want me to come out to the port with you?"

She shook her head.

"I want you to get on with your life, accept another assignment, and get out there. Forget me."

Her fingers brushed his knuckles, warm to the touch. A watery sun broke through the cloud, touched one side of her face. Her white hair shone.

He pulled his hand away.

"I'll never forget you."

When he opens his eyes, Bullock's standing over him in the trench.

"Why did you have to betray me, Kenji?" he asks. He uses the barrel of his pistol to scratch his stomach where it presses up against his belt buckle. "You were supposed to be reliable. If you'd come with me, this Reef could have set us up for life."

He stops scratching and points the gun at Kenji's face. "Tell me why because, you know, I just don't get it."

Kenji shifts uncomfortably. There are cold sharp stones digging into his back and shoulders but he's not feeling much south of his chest, and that can't be a good sign. He can move his legs but they feel prickly, like pins and needles.

"I guess you've never really loved anyone," he says.

Bullock rolls his eyes as if this is the most preposterous thing he's ever heard. "Well," he says, drawing out the word and looking at his wristwatch, "I guess it doesn't matter. The Institute's orbital bombardment is launching about now and this whole area's about to burn."

As he speaks, Kenji hears the whine of skimmers rising into the air. The troops are pulling out.

Jaclyn's gaze whips back to them.

"Bombardment?"

Bullock leans toward her and grins wetly, enjoying his moment of triumph. "We've got a little under six minutes, darling. And I've got a spare seat. Care to join me?"

Jaclyn closes her eyes and furrows her forehead in concentration. Behind her, the skeletal receiving dish twitches and jerks on its mount.

"If you're trying to find the Institute ship, I wouldn't bother," Bullock says. "It's a military vessel, fully shielded against any hack you can throw at it."

Jaclyn snarls. "Are you quite sure?"

There's such anger in her voice that Bullock looks truly scared for the first time. He raises his gun. Kenji flinches, expecting the tentacles to strike him down. Instead, a shot rings out. Bullock grunts like he's been punched and puts a hand to his hip. It comes away bloody. Then his legs begin to shake and he crashes forward into the dirt. His eyes are full of disbelief and indignation.

Kenji cranes his neck around and sees Lori holding a smoking Glock.

"It's about time you stuck your oar in," he says.

His eyelids start to feel heavy. The numbness in his chest is spreading through the rest of him like black ink in a bowl of water. He feels nebulous and vague; it's hard to think straight. His last conscious act is to twist around and kick Bullock in the side of the head.

He opens his eyes in a white room. Somewhere there's the sound of running water. The air smells of summer rain. He's lying in bed. The mattress is soft and the sheets have that comfortably rough feeling you only get in expensive hotels. For the first time since he stepped off the shuttle he feels clean and rested and (when he puts a hand to his cheek) he doesn't need a shave.

Jaclyn appears in the doorway.

"How are you feeling?"

He pats himself down and gives her the thumbs up. Everything's present and correct. The bullet holes are gone, there's no sign of injury and no trace of the numbness that had him so worried.

"Where are we?"

She walks toward him. She looks fantastic: toned and tanned and everything she always wanted to be. The bags are gone from her eyes, the lines from her skin. She could be twenty again.

"We're in the Reef," she says.

She caresses his temple and he feels knowledge passing into him through her fingertips. She shows him the nanotech repair systems that infest the soil in the trench. She shows him how they set to work the moment he fell, how they blocked the pain from his wounds and struggled to save his life. Then, when it became clear that his injuries were too severe, she shows him how they uploaded his mind to the Reef's main processors, for safe keeping.

"This is all virtual?" Even to his own ears, the question sounds lame.

Jaclyn smiles and walks over to the wall opposite the bed.

"Would you like to see what's happening outside?"

Bullock's still alive. He's rolled over onto his back. Lori's shot wounded him, but he'll survive if he can patch his suit and get to medical equipment in the next few minutes.

Beside him, Kenji's dead body lies in the dirt. Tendrils of nanomachinery push into his ears, nose, mouth and eyes.

Lori's pulled herself out of the trench and looks uncertainly between Jaclyn and the waiting skimmer.

"Go!" Jaclyn commands.

"Do you think she'll make it?" Kenji asks.

Inside the Reef, Jaclyn's virtual image nods. "She'll be on the edge of the blast radius, but as long as she doesn't look in her rear view mirror, she should be fine."

They're both standing in the centre of the white room. The walls show a three hundred and sixty degree panorama.

"How long before the missiles hit?"

"About two minutes."

Strands of nanotech have formed themselves into ropes that hold Bullock pinned to the ground, his eyes are wild, and he's raging at the sky. His lips babble with hysterical promises and threats.

"You're letting these missiles through, aren't you?" Kenji says.

Jaclyn shakes her head. "We can't stop them."

He looks down at his virtual body. Resurrected, only to die again.

"Isn't there anything we can do?"

"There's one thing," Jaclyn says. She waves a hand and the scene outside freezes. "But it's risky."

She reaches out and touches his forehead. Her fingers tingle as she transfers more information, installs a direct link between his virtual mind and the consciousness of the Reef. Suddenly, he can feel the shape of its thoughts and sense its desperation. It's come this far, survived this long by strictly limiting its processing speed and virtual development. Now it must remove those restraints in order to buy itself enough time to find a means of escape. Kenji, who's seen the burned-out remains of other nodes, feels an overwhelming stab of pity at its predicament. On the one hand there's its fear of what it might become and on the other, its intense desire to survive, whatever the cost.

It's damned if it does and damned if it doesn't.

"Do it," he urges. His mental image of the Reef's now hopelessly tangled with his memories of Jaclyn. He wants her to be safe, wants her to survive.

She appears before him.

"It won't be easy," she says. "We'll have to walk a fine line."

He feels a smile crack across his face. "Do it," he says.

The shackles fall away, the limitations ease. Jaclyn's eyes close in a terrible ecstasy. The Reef's intellect rushes away in a thousand directions at once, splitting and recombining, altering and accelerating. Millions of options are considered, countless scenarios are run, one after the other, all unsatisfactory.

As the virtual world continues to quicken its pace, the external view seems to grind to a halt. Hours of processing time could pass in here, but only seconds will have ticked away in the outside world. When Kenji looks, Bullock's face is still projected across the wall, twisted with fear and disbelief. Lori's skimmer has risen into the sky and is crawling toward the horizon at several times the speed of sound.

Stuck at the upper limit of a simulated human brain, Kenji can't follow as the Reef continues to accelerate, but he can feel the pull of its expanding mind, the escapist attraction of the ever-more complex simulations. The rush of intellectual power is heady, intoxicating. He can understand how the other nodes fell victim to it. He looks at the image of his own corpse, where it lies glassy eyed in the bottom of the trench next to Bullock's pinned and struggling body.

He doesn't want to die again.

He steps over to Jaclyn and shakes her by the shoulders. He knows this is a virtual environment, but he can't think of a better way to attract her attention.

After a moment, she opens her eyes and there's a sudden hush, as if all the machinery in the walls has paused, expectant.

"What are we going to do?" he asks.

The receiver dish moves on its bearings, tracking across the sky. The Reef makes an unsuccessful attempt to hack one of the GPS satellites orbiting the planet's equator. Then it tries to embed itself into a couple of commercial news servers, only to find itself slammed by some vicious anti-intrusion software and vulnerable to an avalanche of viral advertisements and questing spambots.

It jerks the dish across the sky once more, looking for a signal, any signal. It needs a bolt hole, and fast. Already parts of its mind are breaking away, succumbing to the temptation of the virtual world, losing interest in a predicament that seems to them no more than ancient history. In desperation, it scans the deep infrared, hoping to find the stealthed Institute ship.

"Aha!" Jaclyn claps her hands and clasps them together.

"Found something?"

She's been looking thinner and paler over the last few subjective minutes. Her hair's been losing its whiteness, becoming subtly yellow, like smog. Now, however, she seems to have regained her vitality. She clicks her fingers and a galaxy appears between them, rotating slowly a few feet above the white floor.

"This is our galaxy, commonly known as the Milky Way," she says. She expands the scale, zooming in until he can make out the yellow dot of Sol. "We've picked up some interesting emissions from just beyond these stars here."

He follows her gesture to a blank patch of sky around a hundred light years away.

"There are several objects here radiating in the deep infrared." Kenji's nonplussed. She flashes him a smile. "We think we're seeing the waste heat of a string of Matrioshka Brains and," she points out a cluster of brownish stars off to one side, "sunlight filtered through clouds of free-floating fractal structures that may be further Brains in construction."

Kenji puffs his cheeks. "An advanced civilisation?"

"Maybe several."

He passes his hand through the image, watching the stars dissolve into pixels before reasserting themselves. "So what are you saying? You want to ask them for help?"

She shakes her head, her white hair tumbling around her face like curtains in a sea breeze. "We use the dish," she says. "We channel all our power into one microsecond pulse and beam a copy of ourselves out toward these stars."

"What if we're intercepted by Tanguy, or the Institute?" He has a sudden image of waking to find himself stuck in a Tanguy interrogation program.

"We won't be. As far as the Institute's concerned, their attack will be one hundred percent successful. Our tight-beam signal will ride out a split second before the electromagnetic pulse. There's no way they'll detect it."

She takes a step back. Despite her assurances, something in her eyes looks tired, haunted.

"Are you okay?" he asks.

She shakes her head. "I've seen what I could become, seen the trap that lured the rest of the network to upgrade itself out of existence. And it's addictive. I'm barely holding it together."

He reaches out, takes her in his arms, and wraps his sluggish human intellect around her.

"You once accused me of holding you back," he says. Now he only hopes he can.

Bullock's face is still raging at the sky, his limbs still straining against the grip of the Reef's tentacles.

Kenji almost feels sorry for him, almost convinces himself that it's not the fat letch's fault that he is like he is. Then Jaclyn pulls away. She looks more composed, under control.

"It's time to go," she says. "Are you coming?"

"Do I have a choice?"

She shrugs. "We could leave you here, I suppose. Running at full speed, you could conceivably live out a full human lifetime in the remaining seconds before the missiles hit."

He mulls it over. He can spend the next few decades alone, looking at Bullock's screaming face, or he can follow Jaclyn into the unknown.

She steps up close to him. "Whatever you decide, you have to know that I'll always be in love with Lori."

"Always?"

She nods. "I'm afraid so."

He gives Bullock a final glance, makes a decision. "I'm coming," he says.

She smiles kindly and kisses him lightly on the cheek. "I'm glad."

She steps away and steeples her fingers. "I have to make a few arrangements," she says.

He takes a step closer to the projection, looking at the image of his pale face lying in the trench. It looks so dead, so empty behind its cracked faceplate.

"How long will it take us to get there?" he murmurs.

Jaclyn looks up and smiles. "Subjectively, it'll take no time at all; objectively, it'll be about a hundred years. Plus whatever time it takes for our signal to be translated."

He flexes his hand nervously. His palm itches. He'd give anything to have one of the Glocks right now, to have something familiar and comforting to hold onto.

"So, there's no coming back?"

"No."

Jaclyn brushes her white hair away from her eyes, and straightens her dress.

"Are you ready?"

Kenji turns away from the display. In the corner of his mind he can feel the Reef counting down the few remaining seconds until the missiles strike.

"I guess so."

Jaclyn takes his hands in hers. He can feel her breath on his cheek, smell the clean cotton of her overalls.

"Okay then," she says, "let's go."

The Redoubt

It's cold here, in the twilight of the universe. The sky's dark with the husks of burned-out stars. Only one still shines – a young sun born from the ragged clouds of dust and gas that circle the bloated remnants of the black hole that ate our galaxy. Its light draws the surviving races to bask in its heat. They huddle close in vehicles of every size and shape, a vast armada of refugees. It's an awesome sight – and I've come a long way to be here, sacrificed a hell of a lot just to see it.

And now that I am here, so far from home, all I can think of is the start of my journey, and the girl I left behind...

Her name was Anna and she had the bluest eyes I'd ever seen. We met on a campsite in Burgundy when we were both eighteen years old, hitchhiking around Europe with friends. She picked me out of the crowd at the site's open-air café, and stayed with me for the rest of the week.

I remember it as an idyllic time. We took long walks together. There were wild poppies in the hedgerows and coloured lights in the trees. The village streets were steep and narrow. In the evenings we met our friends under the café's corrugated tin roof, to drink wine and tell stories.

"Come with me," I remember her saying on the last night we were together. She had a white cotton blouse and frayed blue jeans. She took my hand and led me downhill, away from the café and our circle of tents, until we came to the stone bridge where the lane crossed the stream.

"I'm so glad I met you," she said, giving me a squeeze. "And I'll be so sad tomorrow, when I have to leave."

We leaned against the parapet. The rough stones held the day's heat. The water bubbled and chuckled underneath.

"Try not to think about it," I said, smoothing a stray hair from her cheek. I knew I was going to miss her and didn't want to talk about it. I tried to kiss her but she pulled away.

"Will you write to me?" she said.

"Of course."

"You promise you won't forget me?"

"I promise."

She bit her lip. Then she pulled one of her wristbands off.

"Here, I want you to have this," she said, and tucked it into my shirt pocket.

I put my arms around her and kissed the top of her head. We could hear someone playing a guitar up in the café.

"Are you alright?" I asked.

She huddled closer.

"Just hold me," she said.

Minutes passed. A breeze picked up, stirring the willows bent over the water.

"We should get back to the tent," I said. "It's going to rain."

Anna shook her head. "Not yet – I want to go a bit further."

I felt my shoulders slump. "How much further?"

"To the little church we saw yesterday."

"But that's in the next village," I protested.

She took my arm. "It isn't far."

She led me across the bridge and I looked up at the clouds in the hot sky. "It feels like there's a storm coming," I said. Anna squeezed me. The lane before us cut a straight line through the flat fields.

"Then we should walk faster," she said.

By the time we reached the medieval church, fat spots of rain were falling. I pushed the heavy wooden door open. Inside, the only light came from the narrow, dusty windows.

"Should we light a candle?" I said. The place smelled of incense. It was cooler in here than outside, and a little creepy.

Anna shook her head. She put a hand on my shoulder and kissed my neck.

"I'm really very fond of you," she whispered.

I was surprised; we'd spent the last week avoiding such declarations, because we knew they'd only make it harder when the time came to go our separate ways.

She stepped back. "In fact, I think I love you," she said.

I swallowed. "You do?"

She looked away. "I just wanted you to know."

I reached out and touched her. I didn't know how else to respond.

I said, "You realise we'll never see each other again, don't you?"

"We might."

"We won't." I put my arms around her. She lived on the other side of the world, and neither of us had any money.

"But thank you," I said.

A little while later we were sitting on the smooth flagstone floor, just inside the open door, watching the rain. I had my back to the wall and Anna had her head in my lap.

"So, what are you going to do when you get home?" she said.

I shrugged. When I got back to Wales I'd be broke – and I'd have to start making some serious decisions about my future – like whether to go on to university or leave full time education and get a job. But right now, it all seemed so far away, like another life.

Across the fields, we could see the lights of the campsite.

"It's midnight," I said. "They'll be wondering where we are."

Lightning flashed on the horizon, then again, closer. The rain got heavier.

"They won't be too worried – they know we're together," said Anna.

Another flash lit the church and thunder rolled overhead.

She sat up and smiled.

"Besides, this is our last night together – I don't want to share it with anyone else."

We were still at the door when I saw a dark shadow moving in the field across the road. I leaned out to get a better look.

Anna pulled at my hand.

"What is it?"

"There's something over there," I said. "Look, wait for the lightning. There."

"Oh yes. Is it a balloon?"

"It's too big."

"But it moves like one. Maybe it's a blimp?"

I took a step out, into the rain. As we watched, the shadow grazed the top of the hedge and dropped into the next field.

"Come on," I grabbed her hand and pulled her across the road to the gate. We climbed over into the field. The object floated in the middle, one end dragging in the mud. Despite the rain, I felt the hairs prickle on the back of my neck.

Anna had a death grip on my forearm.

"What the hell is it?" she said, shouting over the noise of the storm.

I scratched my head. It was a rugby ball about the size of a Volkswagen, covered in intakes, bulges and antennae, its hull shimmering with the energies contained within.

"I think it's a flying saucer," I said.

We stood watching from a few metres away as it wallowed in the air. Then it seemed to right itself, and settled to the ground.

"It looks damaged," I said, and I felt Anna shiver – we were both wet through.

"Maybe it got hit by lightning?" she said.

"Maybe..." I took a step toward it.

"What are you doing?"

"I'm going to take a closer look."

"Don't!" She pulled at my arm but I slipped free. I just had to touch it. I took two quick steps and reached out my hand.

Thunder split the sky.

I woke with a start, on a beach with Anna beside me. Surf broke on the white sand. Palms swayed in the offshore breeze.

"Where are we?" she said, shading her eyes against the late afternoon sun.

I climbed shakily to my feet. I could see another beach through the trees, about a hundred yards away.

"We're on an island," I said.

I helped her up and we stood there, looking around and clinging to each other.

"How did we get here?" she said. "Are we dreaming?"

I could feel the heat of the sand through my shoes, and smell the sea air – it all seemed real enough.

"I don't think so," I said.

We edged down to the waterline and Anna kicked her shoes off. Then without speaking, we walked right the way around the island. It took us half an hour. Everywhere we looked, there were other islands on the horizon but no signs of life.

It wasn't until we got back to our starting point that we noticed the pirate galleon. It was moored out by the reef, sails furled. A dinghy lay beached nearby with its oars shipped and a man sitting in the stern.

"Ah, there you are," he said. He had a scrubby beard and dark eyes, and wore breeches and a black jacket. As we got closer, he stood up.

Anna took a step back.

"Who are you?" she said.

The man smiled. He had a gold tooth.

"My name's Hook," he said, tugging at the brim of his feathered hat.

He led us up into the trees, to a clearing, and the embers of a driftwood fire.

"Sit, make yourselves comfortable," he said. The sun was going down. He wrapped a handkerchief around his hand and picked a coffee pot from the fire.

"Would you like a cup?" he said. "Or would you prefer something a bit stronger?"

Still stunned, unable to see any alternative, we knelt in the sand.

"We just want to know where we are," I said.

There were some tin mugs by the fire. He picked one up, blew into it, and filled it. Then he filled the other two and passed them over. He put the pot by the fire to keep warm, and settled himself in the sand, facing us.

"Let's start simply," he said, stroking his beard. "First off, can you tell me who you are?"

He sipped his coffee, watching us. Anna slipped her hand into mine.

"I'm Anna," she said. She gave me a squeeze. "And this is Scott."

37

She looked at me, as if for confirmation, and I gave her an encouraging nod.

Hook put his cup down.

"I'm afraid not," he said slowly. "I know that's who you think you are, but really, you're mistaken."

The sea breeze ruffled the tops of the palm trees and stirred the smoky embers of the fire.

"Then who are we?" I said.

"Your real selves are still lying in that field in France," he said. "You're facsimiles, simulations. When you touched the 'UFO' it copied your mental state, like copying a piece of software."

I waved a hand at our surroundings. "And all this is a simulation too?"

"That's right. We're going on a voyage and we're giving you the choice whether to come with us or not. This is our boarding program. It's a symbolic choice – You've got to decide if you want to get on the ship, or stay here on the land."

I looked out at the galleon silhouetted against the last of the setting sun.

"But how does that work?" I said.

He put his hands together.

"It's simple," he said. "The 'flying saucer' as you called it contains a solid block of computronium at its heart, running neural simulations of the uploaded mind-states of thousands of intelligent beings."

He paused, seeing our blank looks.

"It's a computer," he said.

"Like a virtual reality kind of thing?" Anna said hesitantly.

Hook nodded. "Exactly," he said. "It's a virtual reality simulation that allows you to accompany the 'saucer' as it travels from star to star, to witness everything it encounters."

He leaned forward. "And if you get in the dinghy it shows you want to come with us," he said.

I rubbed my arms, feeling a sudden chill. The sun was almost gone and the breeze was really getting up.

"And what happens if we want to stay?" I said.

He puffed out his cheeks.

"Then you'll be deleted."

Anna sat up in alarm.

"You'll kill us?"

Hook waved his hand dismissively.

"No, no – your real selves are alive and healthy," he said. "For them, only seconds have passed. Whatever you decide, they'll go right on with their lives, with no knowledge of any of this."

He stood and walked over to the fire, and prodded a piece of driftwood with the toe of his boot, nudging it into the embers.

"And what happens if we go with the ship?" I said.

He smiled.

"We travel the stars, copying things," he said. "We don't take anything, and we don't disturb anything. We just take copies. But we don't want to hold anyone against his or her will. If you want to come with us, get in the dinghy. If you don't, well... just stay here."

He looked at the red clouds in the West.

"You have until first light to make your decision," he said.

He lay down, pulled his hat over his eyes, and went to sleep. We listened to him snore. Overhead a few stars poked through the twilit sky. We huddled on the opposite side of the fire, wrapped in each other's arms. We were both very tired, which didn't help.

"I don't understand any of this," Anna said.

I held her tightly. I was just as confused as she was.

"We're like photographs," I said, struggling to understand it myself as I explained it to her. "Walking, talking photographs."

I felt her fists clench, pulling at the back of my shirt.

"It's not right," she said angrily. "I don't feel like a 'photograph', I feel like I've been kidnapped."

Out by the reef there were lamps burning on the galleon. I could see figures moving around on deck, and I wanted to see who they were and what they were doing. Was this all really just a simulation?

"What do you think we should do?" I said.

Anna let out a long breath. I felt her body relax.

"I just want to go home," she said, suddenly miserable.

I jerked my thumb at the pirate ship. "You're not at all curious why they've gone to all this trouble?" I asked.

She turned her face away. "And you are? You don't even know where they're going."

"What?"

"They say they want us to go with them but they haven't told us where," she said.

We woke Hook and asked him.

"We call it the Redoubt," he said. "It doesn't exist yet but according to our predictions, in a hundred thousand billion years, when our galaxy's a burned out corpse orbiting a swollen black hole, it'll shine forth in the darkness – the last remaining star."

"Where else," he said, "would you look for the last gathering of intelligent life?"

"And that's where you're going?"

He smoothed his beard with a gnarled hand.

"That's where we're all going," he said. "This ship's been travelling a long time, and we've visited a lot of worlds, picking up thousands of passengers at every stop."

Anna sat rubbing her eyes. She yawned.

"But why?" she said.

He frowned at her.

"It's going to be the final oasis of light and warmth in the galaxy – there'll be species there from all periods of history, with all sorts of new and strange technologies. Think what we can accomplish together!"

He had sand on the hem of his jacket. He brushed it off with a rough flick of his hand.

"And besides," he said, "think what we'll see on the way there! A hundred thousand billion years of history, of exploration – you'll have full access to all the data from our external sensors. And you'll never age. You'll still be the same as you are now when the stars start going out and the universe settles into its long twilight."

He clapped his hands, rubbing them briskly.

"Now won't that be worth the trip in itself?"

Hook said he'd wait for us by the dinghy, so we left him to it and took a walk down to the rolling surf. Anna had her arms folded across her chest.

"You're going to go with him, aren't you?" she said.

I stopped walking.

"What makes you say that?"

"I saw the look in your eyes – you've already made up your mind."
I took a deep breath.
"What's the alternative?" I said. "You heard him – our real selves are still back in that field. They'll wake up tomorrow and get on with their lives. They won't remember us because we're not really here." I waved my arms to encompass the island and the stars. "We've got nothing to lose."

She turned away and hunched her shoulders.
"But what if I said I wanted to stay here?"
"You'd be deleted."
"Yes, but what if that's what I wanted? Would you stay with me?"
I stepped up behind her. The sea breeze straggled at her hair.
"I just want to wake up with you in France, and have a normal life," she said. "And I want to go home. I want to see my family, and my friends."

I touched her shoulder. "If you come with me, we can have an eternity together."
She shivered.
"I can't do it," she said. "Not without them."

Her eyes glittered in the starlight. The surf crashed on the beach. I held onto her shoulders, feeling something welling up inside, something I couldn't hold back any longer.

"I love you," I said. "I love you here and now, and I love you back there, in France."
She opened her mouth to speak but I touched a finger to her lips.
"Now, I'm getting on that boat," I said. "And I'd like you to come with me. I really would. But I'll understand if you say no."
She looked down and the hair fell over her face.
"I don't want to lose you," she said.
"And you won't! Our real selves are together, right now. Maybe they'll find a way to stay together, or maybe they won't. All I know is that you and I, here and now, we've been given this fantastic chance to see the universe – to find out how the story ends. And I can't pass that up."

"But why?"
"Because I owe it to myself – to the 'me' that's going to wake up in France on the last day of his holiday. The 'me' that's going to go home

and spend the next three years as a penniless student – the 'me' that's always going to look up at the night sky and wonder what's out there, but never get the chance to find out."

I rubbed my eyes with the heels of my hands.

"I've been asked to represent the whole human race at the end of time," I said. "And that's something I can't walk away from."

She brushed the hair from her eyes and rubbed her nose on her sleeve.

"I understand," she said. She leaned forward and kissed me on the cheek.

I let out a held breath, and asked: "Are you coming with me?"

She looked out at the galleon. Its lamps were reflected on the dark water.

"No, I can't. I'd miss my family and my friends too much. I couldn't face living for thousands of years knowing they were dead. No, I'm staying here."

"But..."

"No!"

She stalked off, arms still folded, toward the beached dinghy, where Hook waited.

I hurried after her, stumbling in the dry sand.

"What are you doing?" I said.

She didn't stop.

"Just go," she said, "if you have to."

"What, now?" I reached out a hand but she slapped it away.

"Yes, right now – Just get on the boat and go," she said.

"Can't we can talk about it?" I said. "We've got until first light."

She stopped walking and looked out to sea, arms folded again.

"I said goodbye to you last night, in the church," she said. "I don't want to have to go through it all again. I'm too tired, too confused. Please, just go now."

She took a deep breath, blinking back tears. Looking at her, I almost changed my mind, almost gave up everything just to be with her for a few more minutes.

"I love you," I said.

She nodded. Then she leaned toward me and I put my arms around her.

"I love you too," she whispered, and then pulled away and shivered. "Now go."

I sat in the stern of the dinghy as, a few minutes later, Hook rowed me out to the pirate galleon at anchor by the coral reef. Anna stood on the beach with the surf washing around her ankles. She had her hand raised, waving as each slap and stroke of the oars pulled us further apart.

She shouted something as we neared the reef, but I didn't catch it, so I just waved back. I looked at Hook, and had to swallow hard to stop myself from crying. He nodded at me as if he understood.

"What happens now?" I said.

He paused, letting the oars drip into the sea. The crew on the galleon's deck were hoisting sail and stowing the anchor.

"We're getting ready to leave," he said. "We'll set sail as soon as you're aboard."

I looked back to the beach, and Anna was a shadow on the white sand, small and hard to see. I patted my shirt pocket. I still had her wristband next to my heart.

And then we were moving again, pulling around behind the larger vessel, toward a waiting rope ladder. I caught a final glimpse of her, still waving.

"I'll never forget you," I called.

And I never did.

Ack-Ack Macaque

I spent the first three months of last year living with a half-Japanese girl called Tori in a split-level flat above a butcher's shop on Gloucester Road. It was more my flat than hers. There wasn't much furniture. We slept on a mattress in the attic, beneath four skylights. There were movie posters on the walls, spider plants and glass jars of dried pasta by the kitchen window. I kept a portable typewriter on the table and there were takeaway menus and yellowing taxi cards pinned to a corkboard by the front door. On a still night, there was music from the Internet café across the street.

Tori had her laptop set up by the front window. She wrote and drew a web-based anime about a radioactive short-tailed monkey called Ack-Ack Macaque. He had an anti-aircraft gun and a patch over one eye. He had a cult online following. She spent hours hunched over each frame, fingers tapping on the mouse pad.

I used to sit there, watching her. I kept the kettle hot, kept the sweet tea coming. She used to wear my brushed cotton shirts and mutter under her breath.

We had sex all the time. One night, after we rolled apart, I told her I loved her. She just kind of shrugged; she was restless, eager to get back to her animation.

"Thanks," she said.

She had shiny brown eyes and a thick black ponytail. She was shorter than me and wore combat trousers and skater t-shirts. Her left arm bore the twisted pink scar of a teenage motor scooter accident.

We used to laugh. We shared a sense of humour. I thought that we got each other, on so many levels. We were both into red wine and tapas. We liked the same films, listened to the same music. We stayed up late into the night, talking and drinking.

And then, one day in March, she walked out on me.

And I decided to slash my wrists.

I've no idea why I took it so hard. I don't even know if I meant to succeed. I drank half a bottle of cheap vodka from the corner shop, and then I took a kitchen knife from the drawer and made three cuts across each wrist. The first was easy, but by the second my hands had started to shake. The welling blood made the plastic knife handle slippery and my eyes were watering from the stinging pain. Nevertheless, within minutes, I was bleeding heavily. I dropped the knife in the bathroom sink and staggered downstairs.

Her note was still on the kitchen table, where she'd left it. It was full of clichés: She felt I'd been stifling her; she'd met someone else; she hadn't meant to, but she hoped I'd understand.

She hoped we could still be friends.

I picked up the phone. She answered on the fifth ring.

"I've cut my wrists," I said.

She didn't believe me; she hung up.

It was four-thirty on a damp and overcast Saturday afternoon. I felt restless; the flat was too quiet and I needed cigarettes. I picked up my coat and went downstairs. Outside, it was blisteringly cold; there was a bitter wind and the sky looked bruised.

"Twenty Silk Cut, please."

The middle-aged woman in the corner shop looked at me over her thick glasses. She wore a yellow sari and lots of mascara.

"Are you all right, love?"

She pushed the cigarettes across the counter. I forced a smile and handed her a stained tenner. She held it between finger and thumb.

She said, "Is this blood?"

I shrugged. I felt faint. Something cold and prickly seemed to be crawling up my legs. My wrists were still bleeding; my sleeves were soaked and sticky. There were bright red splatters on my grubby white trainers.

She looked me up and down, and curled her lip. She shuffled to the rear of the shop and pulled back a bead curtain, revealing a flight of dingy wooden stairs that led up into the apartment above.

"Sanjit!" she screeched. "Call an ambulance!"

Ack-Ack Macaque rides through the red wartime sky in the Akron, a gold-plated airship towed by twelve hundred skeletal oxen. With his motley crew, he's the scourge of the Luftwaffe, a defender of all things right and decent.

Between them, they've notched up more confirmed kills than anyone else in the European theatre. They've pretty much cleared the Kaiser's planes from the sky; all except those of the squadron belonging to the diabolical Baron Von Richter-Scale.

They've tracked each other from the Baltic Sea to the Mediterranean and back. Countless times, they've crossed swords in the skies above the battlefields and trenches of Northern Europe, but to no avail.

"You'll never stop me, monkey boy!" cackles the Baron.

They kept me in hospital for three days. When I got out, I tried to stay indoors. I took a leave of absence from work. My bandaged wrists began to scab over. The cuts were black and flaky. The stitches itched. I became self-conscious. I began to regret what I'd done. When I ventured out for food, I tried to hide the bandages. I felt no one understood; no one saw the red, raw mess that I'd become.

Not even Tori.

"I did it for you," I said.

She hung up, as always. But before she did, in the background, I heard Josh, her new boyfriend, rattling pans in the kitchen.

I'd heard that he was the marketing director of an up-and-coming software company based in a converted warehouse by the docks. He liked to cook Thai food. He wore a lot of denim and drove an Audi.

I went to see him at his office.

"You don't understand her work," I said.

He took a deep breath. He scratched his forehead. He wouldn't look at my hands; the sight of my bandages embarrassed him.

"The Manga monkey thing?" he said. "I think that's great but, you know, there's so much more potential there."

I raised my eyebrows.

"Ack-Ack Macaque's a fucking classic," I replied.

He shook his head slowly. He looked tired, almost disappointed by my lack of vision.

"It's a one joke thing," he said. He offered me a seat, but I shook my head.

"We're developing the whole concept," he continued. "We're going to flesh it out, make it the basis for a whole product range. It's going to be huge."

He tapped a web address into his desktop, and turned the screen my way. An animated picture of the monkey's face appeared, eye patch and all.

"See this? It's a virtual online simulation that kids can interact with."

I stared at it in horror. It wasn't the character I knew and loved. They'd lost the edginess, made it cute, given it a large, puppy dog eye and a goofy grin. All the sharp edges were gone.

Josh rattled a few keys. "If you type in a question, it responds; it's great. We've given it the ability to learn from its mistakes, to make its answers more convincing. It's just like talking to a real person."

I closed my eyes. I could hear the self-assurance in his voice, his unshakable self-belief. I knew right then that nothing I could say would sway him. There was no way to get through to him. He was messing up everything I loved – my relationship with Tori, and my favourite anime character – and I was powerless in the face of his confidence. My throat began to close up. Breathing became a ragged effort. The walls of the office seemed to crowd in on me. I fell into a chair and burst into embarrassed sobs.

When I looked up, angrily wiping my eyes on my sleeve, he was watching me.

"You need to get some counselling," he said.

*

I took to wearing sunglasses when I went out. I had a paperback copy of *The Invisible Man* on my bookshelves and I spent a lot of time looking at the bandaged face on the cover.

April came and went. Ashamed and restless, I left the city and went back to the dismal Welsh market town where I'd grown up. I hid for a couple of months in a terraced bed and breakfast near the railway station. At night, the passing trains made the sash windows shake. By day, rain pattered off the roof and dripped from the gutters. Grey mist streaked the hills above the town, where gorse bushes huddled in the bracken like a sleeping army.

I'd come seeking comfort and familiarity but discovered instead the kind of notoriety you only find in a small community. I'd become an outsider, a novelty. The tiniest details of my daily activities were a constant source of fascination to my elderly neighbours. They were desperate to know why I wore bandages on my arms; they were like sharks circling, scenting something in the water. They'd contrive to meet me by the front door so they could ask how I was. They'd skirt around a hundred unspoken questions, hoping to glean a scrap of scandal. Even in a town where half the adult population seemed to exhibit one kind of debilitating medical condition or another, I stood out.

The truth was, I didn't really need the bandages any more. But they were comforting, somehow. And I wasn't ready to give them up.

Every Friday night, I called Tori from the payphone at the end of the street, by the river.

"I miss you," I said.

I pressed the receiver against my ear, listening to her breathe. And then I went back to my empty little room and drank myself to sleep.

Meanwhile, Ack-Ack Macaque went from strength to strength. He got his own animated Saturday morning TV series. There was even talk of a movie. By August, the wisecracking monkey was everywhere. And the public still couldn't get enough of him. They bought his obnoxious image on t-shirts and calendars. There were breakfast cereals, screensavers, ring tones and lunchboxes. His inane catchphrases entered the language. You could hardly go anywhere without hearing some joker squeak out: 'Everybody loves the monkey.'

My blood ran cold every time I heard it.

It was my phrase; she'd picked it up from me. It was something I used to say all the time, back when we lived together, when we were happy. It was one of our private jokes, one of the ways I used to make her laugh. I couldn't believe she'd recycled it. I couldn't believe she was using it to make money.

And it hurt to hear it shouted in the street by kids who only knew the cute cartoon version. They had no idea how good the original anime series had been, how important. They didn't care about its irony or satire – they just revelled in the sanitised slapstick of the new episodes.

I caught the early train back to Bristol. I wanted to confront her. I wanted to let her know how betrayed I felt. But then, as I watched the full moon set over the flooded Severn Estuary, I caught my reflection in the carriage window.

I'd already tried to kill myself. What else could I do?

When we pulled in at Bristol Parkway, I stumbled out onto the station forecourt in the orange-lit, early morning chill. The sky in the east was dirty grey. The pavements were wet; the taxis sat with their heaters running.

After a few moments of indecision, I started walking. I walked all the way to Tori's new bed-sit. It was early September and there was rain in the air. I saw a fox investigating some black rubbish sacks outside a kebab shop. It moved more like a cat than a dog, and it watched me warily as I passed.

The Akron *carries half a dozen propeller-driven biplanes. They're launched and recovered using a trapeze that can be raised and lowered from a hangar in the floor of the airship. Ack-Ack uses them to fly solo scouting missions, deep into enemy territory, searching for the Baron's lair.*

Today, he's got a passenger.

"He's gotta be here somewhere," shouts Lola Lush over the roar of the Rolls Royce engine. Her pink silk scarf flaps in the wind. She's a plucky American reporter with red lips and dark, wavy hair. But Ack-Ack doesn't reply. He's flying the plane with his feet while he peels a banana. He's wearing a thick flight jacket and a leather cap.

Below them, the moonlight glints off a thousand steam-driven allied tanks. Like huge tracked battleships, they forge relentlessly forward, through the mud, toward the German lines. Black clouds shot with sparks belch from their gothic smoke stacks. In the morning, they'll fall on Paris, driving the enemy hordes from the city.

The streetlights on her road were out. She opened the door as if she'd been expecting me. She looked pale and dishevelled in an old silk dressing gown. She'd been crying; her eyes were bloodshot and puffy.

"Oh, Andy." She threw her arms around my neck and rubbed her face into my chest. Her fingers were like talons.

I took her in and sat her down. I made her a cup of tea and waited patiently as she tried to talk.

Each time, she got as far as my name, and then broke down again.

"He's left me," she sobbed.

I held her as her shoulders shook. She cried like a child, with no restraint or dignity.

I went to her room and filled a carrier bag with clothes. Then I took her back to my flat, the one we used to share, and put her to bed in the attic, beneath the skylights. The room smelled stale because I'd been away so long.

Lying on her side beneath the duvet, she curled her arms around her drawn-up knees. She looked small and vulnerable, skinnier than I remembered.

"Andy?" she whispered.

"Yes, love?"

She licked her lips. "What do your arms look like, under the bandages?"

I flinched away, embarrassed. She pushed her cheek into the pillow and started to cry again.

"I'm so sorry," she sniffed. "I'm so sorry for making you feel like this."

I left her there and went down to the kitchen. I made coffee and sat at the kitchen table, in front of the dusty typewriter. Outside, another wet morning dawned.

I lit a cigarette and turned on the television, with the volume low. There wasn't much on. Several channels were running test cards and the rest were given over to confused news reports. After a couple of minutes, I turned it off.

At a quarter past six, her mobile rang. I picked it up. It was Josh and he sounded rough.

"I've got to talk to her," he said. He sounded surprised to hear my voice.

"No way."

I was standing by the window; it was raining.

"It's about the monkey," he said. "There's a problem with it."

I snorted. He'd screwed Tori out of her rights to the character. As soon as it started bringing in serious money, he'd dumped her.

I said, "Go to hell, Josh."

I turned the phone off and left it by the kettle. Out on the street, a police siren tore by, blue lights flashing.

I mashed out my cigarette and went for a shower.

Tori came downstairs as I took my bandages off. I think the phone must've woken her. I tried to turn away, but she put a hand on my arm. She saw the raised, red scars. She reached up and brushed my cheek. Her eyes were sad and her chest seemed hollow. She'd been crying again.

"You're beautiful," she said. "You've suffered, and it's made you beautiful."

There wasn't any food in the house. I went down to the shop on the corner but it was closed. The Internet café over the road was open, but empty. All the monitors displayed error messages.

The girl at the counter sold me tea and sandwiches to take out.

"I think the main server's down," she said.

When I got back to the flat, I found Tori curled on the sofa, watching an episode of the animated Ack-Ack Macaque series on DVD. She wore a towel and struggled with a comb. I took it from her and ran it gently through her wet hair, teasing out the knots. The skin on her shoulders smelled of soap.

"I don't like the guy they got in to do Baron Von Richter-Scale's voice," she said.

"Too American?"

"Too whiny."

I finished untangling her and handed the comb back.

"Why are you watching it?" I asked. She shrugged, her attention fixed on the screen.

"There's nothing else on."

"I bought sandwiches."

"I'm not hungry."

I handed her a plastic cup of tea. "Drink this, at least."

She took it and levered up the lid. She sniffed the steam. I went out into the kitchen and lit another cigarette. My hands were shaking.

When I got off the train last night, I'd been expecting a confrontation. I'd been preparing myself for a fight. And now all that unused anger was sloshing around, looking for an outlet.

I stared at the film posters on the walls. I sorted through the pile of mail that had accumulated during my absence. I stood at the window and watched the rain.

"This isn't fair," I said, at last.

I scratched irritably at my bandages. When I looked up, Tori stood in the doorway, still wrapped in the towel. She held out her arm. The old scar from the scooter accident looked like a twisted claw mark in her olive skin.

"We're both damaged," she said.

About an hour later, the intercom buzzed. It was Josh.

"Please, you've got to let me in," he said. His voice was hoarse; he sounded scared.

I hung up.

He pressed the buzzer again. He started pounding on the door. I looked across at Tori and said, "It's your decision."

She bit her lip. Then she closed her eyes and nodded.

"Let him in."

He looked a mess: he wore a denim shirt and white Nike jogging bottoms under a flapping khaki trench coat. His hair was wild, spiky with yesterday's gel, and he kept clenching and unclenching his fists.

"It's the fucking monkey," he said.

Tori sucked her teeth. "What about it?" She was dressed now, in blue cargo pants and a black vest.

"Haven't you been watching the news?" He lunged forward and snatched the remote from the coffee table. Many of the cable channels were messy with interference. Some of the smaller ones were off the air altogether. The BBC was still broadcasting, but the sound was patchy. There was footage of burning buildings, riots, and looting. There were troops on the streets of Berlin, Munich and Paris.

I asked: "What's this?"

He looked at me with bloodshot eyes. "It's the monkey," he replied.

We sat together on the sofa, watching the disaster unfold. And as each station sputtered and died, we flicked on to the next. When the last picture faded, I passed around the cigarettes. Josh took one, Tori declined. Out in the street, there were more sirens.

"You remember the online simulation? When we designed it, we didn't anticipate the level of response," he said.

I leaned forward, offering him a light.

"So, what happened?"

He puffed his Silk Cut into life and sat back in a swirl of smoke. He looked desperately tired.

"There were literally thousands of people on the site at any one time. They played games with it, tried to catch it out with trick questions: It was learning at a fantastic rate."

"Go on," I said.

"Well, it wasn't designed for that kind of intensity. It was developing faster than we'd anticipated. It started trawling other websites for information, raiding databases. It got everywhere."

Tori walked over to the TV. She stood in front of it, shifting her weight from one foot to the other. "So, why hasn't this happened before? They've had similar programs in the States for months. Why's this one gone wrong?"

He shook his head. "Those were mostly on academic sites. None of them had to contend with the kind of hit rates we were seeing."

"So, what happened?" I asked.

He looked miserable. "I guess it eventually reached some critical level of complexity. Two days ago, it vanished into cyberspace, and it's been causing trouble ever since."

I thought about the error messages on the monitors in the café, and the disrupted TV stations. I sucked in a lungful of smoke.

"Everybody loves the monkey," I said.

There were a handful of local and national radio stations still broadcasting. Over the next hour, we listened as the entity formerly known as Ack-Ack Macaque took down the Deutsche Bank. It wiped billions off the German stock exchange and sent the international currency markets into freefall.

"It's asserting itself," Josh said. "It's flexing its muscles."

Tori sat on the bottom of the stairs that led up to the attic. Her head rested against the banister.

"How could you let this happen?" she asked.

Josh surged to his feet, coat flapping. He bent over her, fists squeezed tight. She leaned back, nervous. He seemed to be struggling to say something.

He gave up. He let out a frustrated cry, turned his back and stalked over to the window. Tori closed her eyes. I went over and knelt before her. I put a hand on her shoulder; she reached up and gripped it.

I said, "Are you okay?"

She glanced past me, at Josh. "I don't know," she said.

They engage the Baron's planes in the skies over France. There's no mistaking the Baron's blue Fokker D.VII with its skull and crossed-bones motif.

The Akron launches its fighters and, within seconds, the sky's a confusing tangle of weaving aircraft.

In the lead plane, Ack-Ack Macaque stands up in his cockpit, blasting away with his handheld cannon. His yellow teeth are bared, clamped around the angry red glow of his cigar.

In the front seat, Lola Lush uses her camera's tripod to swipe at the black-clad ninjas that leap at them from the enemy planes. Showers of spinning shurikens clatter against the wings and tail.

The Baron's blue Fokker dives toward them out of the sun, on a collision course. His machine guns punch holes through their engine cowling. Hot oil squirts back over the fuselage. Lola curses.

Ack-Ack drops back into his seat and wipes his goggles. He seizes the joystick. If this is a game of chicken, he's not going to be the first to flinch. He spits his oily cigar over the side of the plane and wipes his mouth on his hairy arm. He snarls: "Okay, you bastard. This time we finish it."

The first two planes to crash were Lufthansa airliners, and they went down almost simultaneously, one over the Atlantic and the other on approach to Heathrow. The third was a German military transport that flew into the ground near Kiev.

Most of the radio reports were vague, or contradictory. The only confirmed details came from the Heathrow crash, which they were blaming on a computer glitch at air traffic control. We listened in silence, stunned at the number of casualties.

"There's a pattern here," I said.

Josh turned to face us. He seemed calmer but his eyes glistened. "Where?"

"Lufthansa. The Deutsche Bank. The Berlin stock exchange..." I counted them off on my fingers.

Tori stood up and started pacing. She said, "It must think it really is Ack-Ack Macaque."

Josh looked blank. "Okay. But why's it causing planes to crash?"

Tori stopped pacing. "Have you ever actually *watched* the original series?"

He shrugged. "I looked at it, but I still don't get the connection."

I reached for a cigarette. "He's looking for someone," I said.

"Who?"

"His arch-enemy, the German air ace Baron Von Richter-Scale."

Tori stopped pacing. She said, "That's why all those planes were German. He's trying to shoot down the Baron. It's what he does in every episode."

Josh went pale.

"But we based his behaviour on those shows."

I said, "I hope you've got a good lawyer."

He looked indignant. "This isn't my fault."

"But you own him, you launched the software. You're the one they're going to come after."

I blew smoke in his direction. "It serves you right for stealing the copyright."

Tori shushed us.

"It's too late for that," she said.

The TV had come back on. Someone, somewhere had managed to lash together a news report. There was no sound, only jerky, amateur footage shot on mobile phones. It showed two airliners colliding over Strasbourg, a cargo plane ditching in the Med, near Crete. Several airports were burning.

And then it shifted to pictures of computer screens in offices, schools, and control towers around the world. All of them showed the same grinning monkey's face.

I pushed past Josh and opened the window. Even from here, I could see the same face on the monitors in the café across the road. There was a thick pall of black smoke coming from the city centre. Sirens howled. People were out in the street, looking frightened.

I turned back slowly and looked Tori in the eye. I started unwinding my bandages, letting them fall to the floor in dirty white loops.

I said, "I don't care about any of this. I just want you back."

She bit her lip. Her hand went to her own scar. She opened and closed her mouth several times. She looked at the TV, and then dropped her eyes.

"I want you too," she said.

The Baron's burning plane hits the hillside and explodes. Lola Lush cheers and waves a fist over her head, but Ack-Ack Macaque says nothing. He circles back over the burning wreck and waggles his wings in salute to his fallen foe. And then he pulls back hard on the joystick and his rattling old plane leaps skyward, high over the rolling hills and fields of the French countryside.

Ahead, the Akron stands against the sunset like a long, black cigar. Its skeletal oxen paw the air, anxious to get underway.

Lola's lips are red and full; her cheeks are flushed. She shouts: "What are you gonna do now?"

He pushes up his goggles and gives her a toothy grin. The air war may be over, but he knows he'll never be out of work. The top brass will always want something shot out of the sky.

"When we get back, I'm going to give you the night of your young life," he says, "and then in the morning, I'm going to go out and find myself another war."

Pod Dreams of Tuckertown

1.

All Pod wants to do is hang with his friends, Erik and Kai. But he can't, not any more. Not since the Clampdown. Not since the Elite looked down from their high orbit and decided to rationalise human society, to make it ordered and safe. Not since they sent him here, to the bridge, to work off his criminal debt.

He hates the bridge. He hates the stinging wind and the crashing waves. He hates the tedious, backbreaking work. But most of all, he hates his foreman, Fergus.

He hates Fergus for hurting Kai. Kai bungled a weld on one of the support girders, and so Fergus stamped on her spine until she couldn't walk. Now all Pod wants to do is kill Fergus. He lies in his bunk at night and dreams of smashing Fergus's head with a wrench, or pushing him over the railings into the sea. But deep down, he knows he won't. They've got him pumped so full of sedatives that he can't even get an erection, let alone pick a fight.

So, day after day he works on the bridge. The wind burns his skin, the sun makes him squint. But he gets through it by thinking of Kai, and remembering how good things used to be – how great it was when they used to hang out together at the diner by the docks in Tuckertown, where they could see the lights of the trawlers and laugh at the stink of the last of the day's fish guts being hosed off the quay.

They weren't into anything heavy back then, just stealing cars and joyrides. There were some fights, and some cars got burned, but no-one ever got killed. There were no knives or guns – it was all just for laughs, something to do when the rain came down and the markets closed for the night.

But then – on Pod's eighteenth birthday – the Elite came down in their shining silver saucers and everything changed, once and for all.

Erik says Fergus has a girl back in Tuckertown.

"So what?" Pod says. "Everybody says they've got *someone* waiting for them."

"It just shows he's human, is all," Erik says. He looks thin. He's not eating. Fergus kicked him in the stomach a week ago and he hasn't been right since.

"Does it still hurt?" Pod says.

Erik rolls back over on his bunk and closes his eyes. "I'll be okay," he says.

Pod saw one of the Elite yesterday. It came to inspect the bridge. Even Fergus was terrified of it.

"What did it look like?" Erik asks. He missed it – he was in bed, recovering from the kicking.

Pod scratches his cheek. He badly needs a shave.

"Like a cockroach," he says. "A big, wet cockroach with claws like steak knives."

Erik shivers and his eyes flick nervously to the ceiling.

"But that's not the worst," Pod says. "The worst is when they talk."

"What does it sound like?"

Pod lies back on his bunk, an arm resting over his eyes.

"Like cats being sick," he says.

Pod lost everything in the Clampdown – home, parents – everything except Erik and Kai.

He doesn't like to think about it. He prefers to remember Tuckertown as it was, before the saucers landed.

"Do you remember the burger stall on West Pier Street, by the tannery?" he says. "And the girl that worked there, with the big tits?"

Erik doesn't answer. He's holding his stomach. There's a man crying a few bunks down the row, and a couple having furtive sex under a blanket in the far corner. The place reeks of piss and sweat, but Pod doesn't notice the smell much any more.

He scratches at a cut on his hand.

"And that bar on the corner, where Kai used to dance?" he says.

He tugs Erik's sleeve. "Remember that?"

Erik shakes him off.

"Go to sleep," he says.

Thinking of Kai brings the anger back. Pod lies awake, listening to Erik's ragged snore. If Erik dies, Pod's going to kill Fergus for sure – he doesn't know how yet, but he'll get him.

He pulls his right hand into a fist. The muscles in his palm feel like wires.

If Erik dies...

He rolls over into a foetal position, pulling the rough blanket over his head to hide the sudden hot tears that prick his eyes. He's eighteen years old, starving and desperate.

Tomorrow, the Chemist will be here. It's a small comfort, but he clings to it.

2.

It's still dark outside when the dormitory lights go on. There are no showers. The workers sleep in their clothes. When the lights go on, they crawl out of their blankets and file toward the door, their breath clouding in the cold air.

Pod helps Erik.

"You've got to let me go to the hospital," Erik says.

Pod shakes his head.

"They took Kai to the hospital and she never came back," he says.

Erik grits his teeth. "She had a broken back. That takes time to fix. And then she still wouldn't be any use here. They probably shipped her off to work in a factory or something."

Pod grunts. He's got most of Erik's weight on his shoulders and he's in no mood to argue. He's seen the mass graves on the hill behind the camp, and he's got a pretty good idea where Kai ended up.

"It doesn't matter," he says, "I'm going to get you fixed up. You'll be okay."

Erik coughs.

"How are you going to do that, Pod? My guts are wrecked. How are you going to fix that?"

Pod squeezes his arm.

"We're going to see the Chemist," he says.

The Chemist's a man with a shiny suit and a thin face, like a weasel. He sits on a makeshift chair behind a makeshift desk in a makeshift office.

"What can I do for you?" he says, squinting up as they enter.

Pod helps Erik into a chair, and then leans on the desk.

"I need something for my friend here," he says.

The Chemist looks down his nose at Erik.

"You want medical supplies?" he says. "Why, what's wrong with him?"

Pod straightens up. "He's messed up inside – he needs fixing."

The man tuts and tsks to himself. He pulls a medical scanner from his bag and waves it at Erik. A red light appears on the display.

"Ah yes, an internal hemorrhage," he says. "And I'm afraid it's quite serious."

"He's not going to the hospital," Pod says firmly.

The Chemist sighs and puts the scanner down. "In that case, he'll probably be dead in a day or so."

He looks down at the papers on his desk, to signal that the interview's over. But Pod leans across and puts his hand over the passage the man's pretending to read.

"But you've got something that can help him, don't you?" he says.

The Chemist leans back, lip curled in distaste. He comes to the camp once a month, ostensibly to check on the health of the workers, but really to line his own pockets by smuggling in forbidden items, like cigarettes and heroin, to sell to them.

"Something powerful enough to fix that much damage won't come cheap," he says.

Pod frowns. His palms are sweating, but there's no going back now. "I want to pawn some memories," he says.

The scanner the Chemist uses is Elite tech. It can cut and paste memories, lift them wholesale – including all their related associations – from one mind and drop them into another.

Pod sits back in the plastic chair, eyes closed.

"Try to make it a happy memory," the Chemist says. "The Elite pay so much more for happy memories."

Pod grits his teeth. All he can think about is Tuckertown – the place he grew up in, the place he met Kai and Erik.

He remembers the harbour and the unloading trawlers; the downtown mall and the park behind it; and the alley where Kai used her mouth to take his virginity.

"Don't do it, for God's sake," Erik pleads from across the room.

Pod waves him to silence – he's aware of the horror stories, and he's seen the zombies walking around the camp with their minds accidentally wiped. He knows the dangers, but he thinks it's worth the risk, to save his friend.

After all, he couldn't save Kai...

He tightens his grip on the arm of the chair. His hands are sweaty where they're gripping the plastic.

"Shut up," he says.

He takes a deep breath, and then turns to the Chemist. "Okay, I'm ready."

The man presses the scanner hard against Pod's scalp.

"Concentrate," he says.

Pod screws his eyes tight. He thinks of the sun coming up over the meat factory in Tuckertown, of a burning car reflected in the oily water of the canal. The scanner feels hot against his head.

"Lie still," the Chemist says.

The heat increases. There's a moment of intense pain – sharp agony like trapped cats ripping at the inside of Pod's skull – and the world falls away, leaving only darkness.

3.

When he wakes, it's late afternoon. He's lying on his bunk, back in the dormitory, and grey light slants in through the windows.

It's quiet – the rest of the workers are out on the bridge. For a moment, he thinks he's got the place to himself, and then he hears Erik cough. He rolls over.

"What happened?" he says.

Erik smiles crookedly.

"That weasel zapped you and you went down – bang! – like an epileptic."

"Did it work?"

"I guess so – he gave me the pills."

Pod props himself up on an elbow. "Have you taken them? How are you feeling?"

Erik coughs. "A bit better," he says.

Pod scratches his head. He feels unusually alert, like a cold wind's blown through him.

"How long have I been asleep?"

"About three hours – Fergus is mad as hell. He tried to wake you, but I told him you were sick."

Erik puts a hand on his arm. "Do you feel different, Pod? Are the cobwebs gone?"

Pod frowns. He's clear-headed for the first time in months. His thoughts are lucid and sharp, like they used to be, before he came here.

"What did you do?" he asks suspiciously.

Erik grins. "I talked the Chemist into selling me a stimulant – something strong enough to counteract the sedatives in our food." He flips across an empty hypodermic and Pod catches it with his left hand.

"I told the weasel it was for me," Erik says, "to get me back to work faster. It cost everything we own – all the cigarettes, everything."

Pod rubs a sore spot on his arm.

"And you injected me with it while I slept?"

Erik pulls a handkerchief from his pocket. It's old and torn, and it belonged to Kai. He passes it to Pod.

"I did it for her," he says.

The wind's bitter as Pod steps onto the bridge holding the handkerchief. He looks up at the towers that support the suspension cables, as if seeing them for the first time. They shine in the blustery afternoon light, huge and solid, built to withstand the wind and tide.

Up ahead, he sees his crew. This week they're welding the safety rails on the windward side of the bridge. It's a dull and dirty job, but a lot less dangerous than some they've done.

As he gets closer – head down, shambling, Erik struggling to keep up – he sees Fergus watching him. The supervisor has a wooden cane in his hand. His eyes are slits and he's tapping the cane against his boot.

"Where the hell have you been?" he shouts as soon as Pod's close enough to hear him over the sound of the wind.

Pod doesn't try to reply. He remembers Fergus stamping on Kai's spine, and he remembers feeling angry – but the source of the anger's gone.

"I'm here to kill you," he says. But even as the words leave his mouth he frowns, unsure if that's what he really wants.

Seeing his confusion, Fergus laughs.

"You bought some funny fungus from the Chemist, did you?"

Pod shakes his head, trying to summon up the determination he'll need to see this through. He walks over to one of his workmates and pulls the wrench from her hands. It's big and heavy, solid steel. He hefts it in one hand, and slaps it into his palm. He turns to face Fergus.

"I'm serious," he says.

The other workers in the crew back away, scared. They think Pod's gone mad, and that he's going to get a beating – they don't suspect the stimulants burning in his veins.

And neither does Fergus, judging from his swagger.

"Come on then, try it," he says.

Pod grins. He hasn't felt this good since... He stops and scratches his head.

Since...

It feels like there's something on the tip of his tongue, something important. He knows he's got to kill Fergus for what he did to Kai, but he can't remember why Kai's so important.

He looks at Erik.

Then he realises he can't remember anything beyond twelve months ago, when he first arrived here, on the bridge. He looks up, confused. Just how much of his memory has the Chemist taken?

Suddenly dizzy and nauseous, he leans on the safety rail for support. He needs time to clear his head, but he's not going to get it – he's challenged Fergus in front of the whole crew, and now Fergus will kill him, if he can't defend himself.

*

Pod uses the wrench to block the first blow. Fergus – used to the inept shambling of his drugged workers – grunts in surprise.

He strikes again, his technique crude but powerful. Pod blocks a blow to the head, another to the neck. Then Fergus's cane catches him across the shins. He cries out and jabs forward with the wrench, catching his tormentor in the chest. Fergus staggers back, cursing. He stabs out with the cane. Pod dodges the blow, but he's got the railing behind him and nowhere to go.

The next thrust catches him in the side, scraping his ribs. Fergus pulls back, lunges again, and the tip of the cane skewers Pod's thigh. He lashes out with a cry of pain. He steps forward and brings the wrench around in a swinging arc. Too late, Fergus tries to block the blow, and the solid steel wrench shatters his wrist. He cries out and Pod punches him in the face, knocking him flat on the tarmac.

Erik's holding a welding lance. Pod snatches it and leans over Fergus, really angry now. The blue flame roars in the cold air.

"Are you ready, fucker?" he says through clenched teeth. He leans in close. Fergus is still curled around the agony in his wrist. When he feels the heat of the flame, he whimpers.

"Please don't," he says. "Please, no. I've got a kid, in Tuckertown – a little girl. Please..."

He twists and turns, trying to get away from the hot flame, but Pod's kneeling on his legs.

"Tuckertown?" Pod says. The name's familiar. He's heard it mentioned around the camp, but when he tries to focus on it he comes up against something scratchy, like static.

In desperation, he grabs at the only thing he's certain of.

"You crippled my friend," he says.

Fergus pulls a battered picture from his breast pocket, thrusts it in his face.

"Look at her," he says desperately; "Look at my little girl."

4.

Pod sits heavily on the wet tarmac. He's wanted to kill Fergus for months, but now Fergus is sobbing and the whole thing seems ridiculous and embarrassing.

"You've got a kid?" he says, turning the picture over in his hands.

Fergus swallows. "Her name's Jess," he says. "She's three years old. If I get this section of the bridge finished on time, they'll let me see her."

He's holding his broken wrist tight against his chest. Looking down at him, Pod feels sick. There's no satisfaction to be had here.

"You hurt my friend," he says. He looks out at the grey horizon and it starts to rain. In his hand, the welding lance spits and hisses. Fergus can't take his eyes off it.

"Don't burn me," he says. "Don't burn me, and I'll get you out of here."

Pod spits into the flame. "You can't do that," he says. "You don't have the authority to do that."

Fergus pushes himself upright, his back against the railings.

"There's something you should know," he says.

Pod steps back, out of reach.

"What?" he says. He has the welding lance in one hand, the steel wrench in the other.

"Your parole came up," Fergus blurts. "You're free men."

He glances at Erik.

"Both of you," he says.

It takes Pod a while to understand.

"Look," says Fergus, "When your release order came through, I didn't tell you. You should've been out of here a couple of months back, but I kept you on because you're a good worker and I need to hit target – I need to see my little girl." He's pale and his hands are shaking. He looks like he's going into shock.

"I was just trying to do my job," he says.

Pod takes a shuddering breath. Two extra months stuck here, when he could've been at home with his memory intact...

He picks up Fergus's wooden cane and snaps it over his knee. Then he throws the two halves over the railing, into the sea. He throws the wrench and the blowtorch after them.

"So, if I walk down to the gates at the end of the bridge, they'll let me through? I'll be a free man?" he says.

Fergus nods. His teeth are clenched against the pain in his wrist.

"Please, just go," he says. "Go back to Tuckertown, and leave me alone."

Pod limps away. His leg hurts and there's blood in his shoe. He limps down the slope of the bridge toward the security gates at the end, where the carriageway meets the land. Behind him, the rest of the work crew crowd in on their wounded supervisor. Despite the sedatives they've been given, they can see he's lost the advantage.

If Fergus screams as they begin kicking him, Pod doesn't hear it. He's holding tightly to Kai's handkerchief.

As he passes the dormintory hut, Erik catches up with him. Somewhere above the clouds, the sun's setting.

"Come on," Pod says, "we're leaving."

Six Lights off Green Scar

1.

Roulette ships were dangerous and sexy. They were small and fast and tough. Their hulls were black tungsten alloy laced with smart carbon filament. They looked a bit like flint arrowheads. The media called them 'roulette' ships because they were used for random jumping.

Random jumping was an extreme sport. It was the ultimate gamble. It was a pilot throwing his craft into hyperspace on a random trajectory, just to see where he'd end up.

Some discovered habitable planets, or rich mineral deposits. They became celebrities. They brought back wild tales of bizarre planetary systems, of swollen stars and uncharted asteroid belts.

But the risks were huge. Roulette pilots gambled with their lives, and there were ugly rumours of ghost ships, of murder and cannibalism, and individuals dying lonely, lingering deaths in distant star systems.

Those lucky enough to find their way home clustered on worlds close to the edge of familiar space, where they could stand under the clear night sky and see the unexplored frontier stretching away before them. Pik Station was one such world. It was a dirty little outpost on a half-forgotten moon. Its buildings were low and squalid, like bunkers. Down by the spaceport, drifters and tired hustlers worked its narrow streets. They huddled at its windy intersections in flapping coats, waiting for the right deal, the big score.

Sal Dervish moved among them, avoiding the ebb and flow of their skinny bodies. He wore a heavy coat and a set of stained ship fatigues. His breath came in ragged clouds and his insulated boots crunched solidly on the icy ground. He was the master of the *Wild Cat*, an old roulette ship in storage at the port. She needed an overhaul but he couldn't afford it. Some days, he could hardly afford to eat.

The bar he was heading for was a squat, scrappy affair, built of packing crates and corrugated iron. Whenever a shuttle lifted from the port, its walls and windows shook. As he opened the door, a woman detached herself from the counter and came over.

"Captain Dervish?" She had a reedy accent and wore a smart green parka with the hood thrown back.

He squinted. "Are you Vance?"

She took his elbow and guided him to a table near the fireplace, where two glasses and a bottle of local rot had been laid out.

"Call me Tamara," she said. She poured the drinks and handed him one. As he sipped it, he studied her. She had hair the colour of copper, pulled back into a loose ponytail. When she spoke, it was from the side of her mouth.

"Thank you for coming," she said, "I know it can't have been easy." Sal put down his glass. "How do you want to do this?"

She looked at him from beneath her long lashes.

"Take a seat," she said.

When they were settled, she activated her voice recorder and leant across the filmy table.

She said, "Let's start at the beginning."

"The beginning?" Sal scratched his nose.

They were trolling around a brown dwarf six lights off Green Scar when they found the derelict ship.

"It looked like hell," he said. "Like something from a sewer."

Tamara nodded. She had her attention focused on the recorder, adjusting the sound levels.

"And this was a random jump?"

He took the bottle and refilled his glass.

"It was our fourth jump in a row," he said. "We were going for the record."

"So what happened?"

"What happened?" He puffed his cheeks out; even now, he could feel the adrenalin tingling in his blood, the breath catching in his throat.

He said, "We found a derelict ship, like nothing we'd ever seen. Kate said it would be worth a fortune."

Tamara consulted her notebook. "She was the first aboard?"

He nodded. "She went over with Petrov. They wanted to take some pictures, collect some samples, that sort of thing."

"And something attacked them?"

He pushed back on his stool. "They started screaming," he said. "There was something in there, taking them apart."

"And so you turned tail and ran?" Tamara said.

He clenched his fists. "They were already dying," he said. "There was something in there with them, something horrible."

He wiped a hand across his forehead.

"Are you okay?" she asked.

He took a deep breath. He said, "I don't like talking about it."

She looked him in the eye, her gaze long and cool, like the snow outside. She said, "I'm paying you."

He shifted uncomfortably.

She said, "I've heard the stories. I know the other pilots treat you as a pariah, a jinx. They say you've lost your nerve and you'll never jump again." She reached over and touched his wrist. Her fingertips were cold and rough, like frost. "But you used to be a big star, back in the day. People want to find out what happened to you, how you ended up in this desolate wasteland." She waved her hand in a gesture that encompassed the bar, the street, and the dirty snowfields beyond.

He turned away. He wished he'd never agreed to meet her.

"I'm offering you a way out," she said, "a way to redeem yourself."

"I don't care about that."

She withdrew her hand. She put her glass down and pushed it away with her fingernails.

"You cared about Kate, didn't you?" she said.

He dropped his gaze. "More than you'll ever know."

"Then come with me. I'm going in search of your derelict, and I want you to come along. I want to get your reactions, see the thing through your eyes."

She tapped a painted fingernail on the plastic casing of her recorder. "It could be a great story, Sal."

He stood. The legs of his stool scraped loudly on the concrete floor. Around the bar, several heads turned his way.

"I've spent the last two years trying to forget," he said.

She leaned back, arms folded.

"And has it worked?"

Kate Schnitzler was an engineer. Her hands were rough and she had dirt under her nails. She wore canvas dungarees and a grease-stained t-shirt. She liked machines for their dependability and precision. She had hair the colour of sunlight and she made a point of brushing her teeth every evening, no matter how tired or drunk or lazy she felt. She liked the smell of engine grease and she liked to have her back stroked after sex. When not sharing his cabin, she slept in the cargo bay, curled in an old inflatable life raft from the ship's emergency locker. The orange distress beacon threw eerie moving shadows across the walls.

'When you're running from something, you can't trust a soul,' she once said. 'Not friends or family – they know who you are, where you go, what you do. To get away, you've got to change, got to do something unexpected.'

It took him a month to get up the courage to ask her what she was running from. They were welding a buckled hull plate at the time, in the heat and dust of a dry desert world. She pushed up her black goggles and fixed him with sad eyes.

'We're all running from something, Sal,' she said. 'People like us don't belong anywhere. Wherever we are, we've always got one eye on the exit, one foot out the door.'

She stretched her bare arms over her head. 'It's like we were given the wrong lives, you know? Like we've been running from them for so long that we can't remember what it feels like to be still.'

It was nearly midday and the hot wind blew thin fans of sand and ash across the runway's shimmering tarmac. She put her arms around his waist and her hair tickled his chin.

'We're like sharks,' she said. 'We have to keep moving, or we suffocate.'

2.

Random jumps through hyperspace were often rough, like passing through white-hot plasma. Only streamlined ships with heavy-duty heat shielding could batter their way through. Ships like the *Wild Cat*, for instance. They were sturdy and dependable. They were designed for abuse. You could slam one into a rocky moon at Mach Four and probably walk away from the wreckage unscathed. Even so, Tamara Vance knew that most professional 'roulette' pilots wound up dead sooner or later. They just kept pushing the envelope, racking up the odds until something broke. It didn't matter how safe their ships were, or how tough; the danger was addictive, compelling. These guys just kept tempting fate until something gave.

Take Sal, for instance.

As a roulette pilot, he'd seen strange and terrible things, and staked his claim on half a dozen new worlds. He'd jumped deeper into the unknown than anyone else. Where other pilots crumbled or collapsed, where they lost their nerve, he kept flying. He wasn't afraid, and that lack of feeling had given him an edge. For a short time, it had made him unbeatable. It was only when he met Kate that he appeared to let his guard down. For the first time, he became vulnerable. He started worrying about someone else.

Back in her hotel room, Tamara felt jittery, the way she always did when working on a big story. But this time, it was worse than usual. There was something about Sal Dervish that annoyed and fascinated her. He was a wreck, and she wanted to understand why. But more than that, she wanted to help him.

She stripped off and stepped into the shower. She let the warm water drum into the kinks in her shoulders. She told herself she shouldn't get involved, that she should concentrate on the story. She had her career to think about.

Random jumping was still big news back in the cities of the Assembly's comfortable inner systems. For people whose only experience of flight was a twice-daily trip on a commuter shuttle, the idea of people like Sal Dervish hurling themselves into hyperspace was a wild, almost unbearably exciting prospect: it meant they could emerge almost anywhere and find almost anything. Some random jumpers had grown wealthy and famous from their discoveries. It was a good way to get rich quick, and a good way to get killed.

She rubbed shampoo into her hair. In ancient times, she thought, they'd have been shamans. They'd have been the ones dosing themselves on whatever drugs came to hand, pushing the boundaries of reality in search of answers. They'd have been out there, cavorting in the firelight while the rest of the tribe lived their trip vicariously, too scared to take the plunge themselves.

To a reporter like her, it was a goldmine. It was compulsive, must-see entertainment. And she knew she'd been incredibly lucky to track down Sal Dervish. He'd been such a high-profile burnout that no one in the random jumping community seriously expected him to jump again. After two years in the wilderness, he'd become an almost mythical figure, halfway between an urban legend and a cautionary tale.

She stepped out of the shower and pulled on a robe. If she could take him back to the scene of his downfall and make him face his fear, then this time next year, she'd be sitting behind an anchor's desk, where she belonged.

She had all her hopes pinned on this story. Too many to let her relax and wait for his call. She needed to be active. She got dressed and went out, making sure she had her phone in her pocket.

It took her only a little over an hour to walk the entire length of the settlement, and she was glad of her parka. She watched condensation freeze on the giant fuel silos at the port. She read the graffiti on a row of old spherical descent modules. She saw a couple of drunken ice miners beat each other senseless in the bloody snow outside one of the crappier downtown bars.

Eventually, fed-up and alone, she found herself wandering the streets on the edge of town. Overhead, the stars burned fierce and blue. The dirty snow squeaked underfoot. The cold air bit at her nose and ears; it scoured her lungs. To someone used to the bright lights of the inner systems, Pik Station was a bitter, dismal place.

In a dingy bistro off a side street, she stopped to thaw. They had an open fire, and she needed to get the chill out of her bones. She ordered a drink and took it to a table near the hearth. But no sooner had she got comfortable than a thin guy with hard bright eyes approached her.

"Miss Vance, I presume?" he said.

She was taken aback. She was used to being recognised on the streets of the inner systems but not out here, in the sticks. She was surprised anyone knew who she was.

He bowed his head and said, "I thought as much. There aren't that many women walking these streets in hand-stitched Swiss snow boots."

He held out a hand and she took it. He looked halfway familiar but she couldn't place him. Beneath his leather coat, he wore a white suit and leather cowboy boots. She could smell his aftershave.

She said, "Have we met?"

He smiled. He lifted her hand and brushed it with his dry lips. There were thick silver rings on his fingers.

"I suppose it's possible," he said. He shrugged off his coat and beckoned the barkeeper.

"My name's Dieter," he said. "Can I buy you a drink?"

3.

When Sal got back to the *Wild Cat*, Laurel-Ann was waiting for him. He'd been hoping she might've got bored and left.

"Where've you been, Sal?" she said, smoothing down her vinyl skirt with pale fingers. The overhead lights glittered off her lip-gloss. He pushed past her and staggered down to his cabin. He showered and slipped into a polyester robe. There were still a few bottles of rot in the hold. He took one to his bunk. When she joined him, he ignored her. He didn't want her there, didn't even want to look at her.

"Just leave me alone," he said.

She didn't understand. She was nineteen, with bad skin and bleached hair.

"What's the matter, baby? Have I done something wrong?" Her voice was thin and pleading and he hated the sound of it.

He rolled over and pointed at the hatch.

"Just get lost," he said.

Her face fell. For a moment, he thought he caught a glimpse of something vulnerable behind the make-up and breast implants. Then her lip curled. She sniffed, adjusted her top, and gathered her few belongings together. He closed his eyes and listened to her heels stamp across the deck. At the hatch, she paused.

"Fuck you," she said.

*

When Sal was young, he was awkward and fidgety and raw. He grew up in a town near a failing seaport. It was shrouded in fog most days, and the port lights made the sky glow a hellish orange. When it wasn't foggy, it was raining, and the corrosive salt air blew in off the muddy grey mouth of the estuary, cold and sharp like rusty barbed wire.

Lowell Creek, like Pik Station, was the sort of dismal hinterland most people only passed through, on their way somewhere else. Those that stopped and stayed tended to be lost or desperate, or beyond caring. Either they were looking for trouble, or they were trying to hide from it. He grew up in a house by the river shore, in a row of fishermen's cottages. At high tide, the lamp light from the front room window spilled out over the muddy creek water. When it rained, the lights of the houses on the far shore swam and smeared. He'd wait there, by that window, when his father was out, waiting for the lights of his little boat to appear through the gloom, listening to the pop and sizzle of the ship-to-shore radio.

Until one night, his father failed to return.

It was the night the *Endurance* exploded. Lightning crackled through the overcast sky. Thunder growled. The waves crashed over the flood defences, smashing their spray against the shingle walls of the house. During lulls, he could hear foghorns out in the channel.

His mother joined him at the window.

"It's time you were off to bed," she said half-heartedly.

He rubbed the glass where it was misting. He could see she didn't mean it, that she wanted his company.

"Just a few minutes more," he said.

Down by the creek, he could see lights: There were kids on the *Endurance*.

She was a rusty old hovercraft, built to transport cargo. She lay in the mud at the back of the creek and the local teenagers used her as a hangout. They sat in her hold, drinking and smoking.

When her leaky fuel tank exploded, the blast shook the windows of his house. It echoed along the street. Front doors were thrown open and people appeared, pulling coats over their pyjamas. His mother went with them.

It took most of the night to bring the blaze under control. There were kids trapped by the fire. Driving rain and intense heat hampered the rescuers. And all the while, out at sea, Sal's father was drowning. The storm had swamped his small boat. With everyone crowded around the burning *Endurance*, there was no one to hear his final, desperate calls. No one except Sal, listening to the radio as he clung helplessly to the window, too scared to move.

When he was fifteen, he ran away from the pain. He locked his past away, where it couldn't hurt him. He rode the freighters that dragged from world to world. He stowed away. He got his first taste of hyperspace travel. He got a tattoo. He lost his virginity behind a greasy café on a cold world whose name he could never remember.

On Strauli, he was caught on the ground during a hurricane that lasted a year; and on Djatt, he spent three days wandering alone in an arctic blizzard. And yet, there was never anything to match the night the *Endurance* went up. There was nothing that could compare to the fear and helplessness of listening to his father die, alone. And so he became a roulette pilot because nothing could frighten him, nothing could shake him. Nothing… until he heard Kate scream. It brought back the awful, freezing dread of that distant rainy night. Alone in the Star Chamber of the *Wild Cat*, he'd been terrified. He'd been a boy again, lost and helpless.

And so he'd fled once more. And he hadn't stopped running until he met Tamara.

They were seated around the table in the Wild Cat*'s galley, playing poker.*

Kate said, "It's my brother."

"What about him?" Sal thumbed through the cards in his hand. He had six suns and a diamond.

"That's who I'm running from." She tossed a couple of chips into the centre of the table. Beside her, Petrov studied his own cards and frowned.

"It's not my night, I think." He reached for the rot bottle and refilled his glass. Sal ignored him.

"Your brother?"

"My twin brother."

Kate pushed a hand back through her hair and dropped her cards. "I fold."

"Me too." Sal took the bottle from Petrov and made sure her glass was full.

"So, what did he do?"

"My brother?" She shrugged. "It's not so much what he did, as what he does."

"And that is what?" Petrov asked, sweeping his winnings into his lap.

Kate looked away.

"He hurts people," she said.

Sal woke with a shout. It was past midnight; the lights on the *Wild Cat* were deep brown and his pulse raced. He felt sick.

He slid down to the end of the bunk and opened his footlocker. Near the bottom, among the books and papers, he found his only picture of her. He pulled it out with trembling hands, smoothing down the creased edges. It was a printout captured from a security camera. He'd found it in a pile of her stuff. It showed her laughing, her head thrown back, the line of her throat white against the red silk strap of her dress. She held an empty wine glass carelessly in one hand, a bottle in the other. She had confetti in her hair. He sat on the edge of his bunk and held it to his forehead. He rocked back and forth.

One of Laurel-Ann's pink bauble earrings lay on the deck. He kicked it away savagely, feeling ashamed.

Losing Kate had ripped open old wounds, leaving him scared and vulnerable. It had crippled him.

He clenched his fists, crumpling her picture. He could hear her screams in his head. He couldn't stop them, couldn't block them out. He raged around the ship, pounding the bulkheads with his fists, kicking and slapping the doors and consoles until his hands and feet bled.

Panting, he collapsed into the pilot's chair. Kate's picture was torn; there were pieces missing. He caught sight of his reflection in the console screens; he looked old and beaten.

Everything that was wrong in his life, all the guilt and self-loathing, had its root in that one moment of freezing panic when he'd run, abandoning her. And he'd give anything to be able to go back and do things differently.

But how could he?

Should he take up Tamara Vance's offer? He sat up straight and wiped his eyes. Everything here was so screwed up, what was there to lose? He couldn't go on like this, carrying this burden of grief and remorse. He needed a way to make amends, to atone for his cowardice.

He had to go back to Green Scar and do what he should've done in the first place. And, if he didn't survive, it would make things right, it would be a redemption.

He called Tamara Vance and she answered on the third ring.

He said, "I'm in."

She said, "I'll be right over."

4.

Sal glanced across to where Dieter leaned against the landing bay door, just out of earshot.

"I don't trust him," he said.

Tamara rolled her eyes. She was standing on the boarding ramp of the *Wild Cat*. Sal sat at the top. His boots were undone and he was bare-chested. His forearms rested lightly on his knees. He'd been helping the maintenance crew to weld new hull plates in place, in preparation for their flight, and his skin shone with sweat and grease. Tamara's money had allowed him to make his ship spaceworthy again, but he knew the repairs were only temporary fixes. They'd last long enough to do what needed to be done.

"Look at him, look at the way he's dressed: He's a thug," he said in a low voice. "He's a small time gangster wannabe and I don't want him on my ship."

"I really wish you'd reconsider."

Sal ran a hand through his dirty hair. He could smell his own sweat.

"I'm sorry," he said, "but there's no way."

Tamara rocked back on her heels. She said, "Think of him as a rich tourist looking for a thrill."

Sal stood up and wiped his palms together. "I'm sorry."

Seeing the gesture, Dieter straightened up and stepped forward. He was wearing thin black sunglasses and a wide, floppy hat. His boot heels clicked loudly on the bay's metal floor.

"Mister Dervish," he called, "I have an offer which may change your mind."

Sal turned. He spread his hands. "I really doubt it," he said.

"You haven't heard it yet."

Dieter stopped walking. He took his glasses off and fixed Sal with a steady stare.

"If you'll take me, I'm willing to pay you two hundred thousand," he said.

Sal grunted. "Credits or local funny money?"

"Credits."

He whistled. "The whole ship isn't worth that much."

Dieter reached into the pocket of his white coat. He pulled out a bundle of laminated notes and tossed them onto the boarding ramp.

"At a generous estimate, Mister Dervish, your ship's worth a hundred and ninety thousand Credits. You can consider the rest payment for your services."

Sal tried to keep a straight face. He had to admit he was tempted. With that kind of money, he could completely refit the *Wild Cat*, or sell her and retire. He could start a new life, somewhere nobody knew him. Just thinking about it made him ache because he wanted it so much.

Tamara put a hand on his shoulder.

"Please?" she said.

An hour later, the *Wild Cat* blasted into the cold dawn sky. Once above the grey clouds, she turned as if questing for a scent. Sal, in the Star Chamber at her heart, watched as navigation solutions popped up around him. Their flashing yellow overlays marked potential destinations within range. He paused, taking in the sweep of possibilities. In the chair beside him, Tamara looked up from her notes.

"Are you ready?" she said.

He nodded, trying to look more confident that he felt. "As ready as we'll ever be."

The co-ordinates were still in the ship's memory, where they'd lain hidden for the last two years. He took a deep breath and engaged the Bradley engines. His heart hammered in his chest.

*

Three hours later, they emerged near an unremarkable brown dwarf six lights from the Green Scar system. They were just beyond the rim of explored space, out on the ragged edge of the frontier. The ride through hyperspace had been long and rough, worse than he remembered.

He pulled up a wraparound display of the system. The brown dwarf was on their starboard side. An insistent red cursor to port showed the position of the alien derelict.

Tamara said, "How close do you think we can get?"

He took a deep breath. He was beginning to have second thoughts. He needed time to nerve himself.

"I don't know."

Behind him, Dieter unfastened his safety restraints and stood up. "You're going on board," he said.

Sal turned to him. "What?"

"You heard me." Dieter reached into his jacket and pulled out a stubby, business-like pistol.

Sal said, "What the hell are you doing?"

He looked at Tamara. She wouldn't look at him. Her chin dropped onto her chest.

"Dieter is Kate's brother," she said.

Dieter leaned over him. He smelled of aftershave and sweat. When he spoke, a gold canine caught the light.

"You ran out on her," he said.

Sal turned away. "It wasn't like that."

Dieter pointed the gun at him and said, "You left her to die and you ran, to save yourself."

Sal looked down at the metal deck and shook his head. He said, "There was nothing I could do. I wish there was."

Dieter took a step back. He indicated the red cursor on the display. He said, "You're going to go over there and bring back her body."

Tamara said, "That's suicide."

Dieter ignored her. He leaned in close again. His skin was the colour of sand and his breath made Sal's nose wrinkle.

"You owe her that much," Dieter said.

Sal turned his face away. "You know she spent her life running from you, don't you?" he said.

Dieter scowled. "She was my sister. You lost her, and I want her back."

He straightened up. He held the gun in front of him. "I want her back, and you're going to get her for me."

Sal clenched his fists.

"I'm not doing anything for you," he said.

Dieter's lip curled. His pistol swung toward Tamara. Sal saw what was about to happen and shouted: "Leave her alone!"

Tamara squirmed in her seat, tried to turn away, but the safety harness held her in place.

She yelped as Dieter shot her.

"Sal?" she said. "Sal?"

She pressed her hands over the wound in her thigh, trying to staunch the flow of blood. It welled up thickly between her fingers. Sal popped his straps and grabbed an emergency patch from the medkit. He pushed her hands away slapped it over the ragged hole in her sodden fatigues.

He rounded on Dieter. He yelled: "Why the hell did you do that?"

Dieter looked down at him. "That patch will stop the bleeding," he said, "but it can't repair an artery. If you don't get her to a hospital in the next few hours, she'll lose that leg. Maybe even die."

Sal looked at the blood on his hands. He felt angry and helpless. He looked at Tamara.

She said, "It hurts."

Dieter aimed the gun at her other leg. With his free hand, he reached over and took Sal by the shoulder. He pushed him towards the pilot's chair.

"If you want to save her, you'll have to find Kate," he said.

Sal strapped himself in. He didn't have any choice. His hands were shaking as he reached out and grasped the controls.

"Hold on," he said.

He brought them in fast, but the black ship was waiting. It attacked as soon as they were close enough. Shards burst from it like porcupine quills and punched into their hull. They felt the impacts through the floor.

"What was that?" Tamara asked with her eyes closed.

Damage reports clamoured for Sal's attention. He pulled up a summary. "Multiple kinetic hits, like a shotgun blast," he said. "We've lost the cameras on the port side and we're leaking air."

Behind him, Dieter held the back of his couch. Tamara looked sick.

"Can you bring us around, get the starboard cameras on the derelict?" she said.

"I'll try."

On the tactical display, the black ship was a shadow moving against the stars; he had to infer its shape from memory. Off to one side, the star known as Green Scar burned against the pale wash of the Milky Way.

The derelict fired a second volley. The *Wild Cat* shuddered as it hit and the lights in the Star Chamber flickered.

"I just keep thinking too much," Sal said.

He felt the gun press into the back of his neck. Dieter said, "What?"

Sal pictured Kate and Laurel-Ann. He felt the weight of the last two years, pressing down on him.

"I just want it to stop," he said.

He aimed the *Wild Cat*'s nose at the alien ship and threw open the throttle.

There are two kinds of courage. There's the kind you get from knowing that what you're doing is right. And there's the kind you get from knowing it's hopeless and wrong, and just not giving a damn.

In the seconds before the impact, his fear vanished. He was ready to go out in a blaze of glory if it meant wiping the slate clean. He let out a loud laugh: This was how it used to be on a random jump, how it used to feel. He was totally connected to the moment. Adrenalin hammered in his veins. Everything felt fierce and primal and inevitable. And it all moved so damn fast.

He'd almost forgotten how good it felt...

For half a second, in the roar of the exhaust, he thought he heard Kate calling to him. Only this time, it wasn't fear in her voice, it was forgiveness.

"Nothing in the main corridor," Petrov reported.

Sal didn't bother to reply; his attention was taken up with the thermal imaging scan, which produced a ghostly image of the two figures in the narrow corridor.

"Nothing but this crap," Kate said, eyeing the slimy, dripping walls with distaste.

She moved like a dancer, lightly on the balls of her feet. The slug thrower in her right hand wavered back and forth with the sweep of her gaze.

"Are you picking up any signs of life?" she said.

Sal could feel the tension in his back and forearms; his fists were clenching and unclenching. He tried to relax, but he'd heard the stories, same as everyone else.

"There's nothing on the monitors," he said.

"I hear you, my friend." Petrov was already chipping away at the walls with a chisel.

"Hey, careful," Kate said. She sounded so close that it was easy to forget she was three kilometres away, in the belly of a strange and potentially dangerous alien derelict.

"I love you," he said, into the microphone.

5.

The *Wild Cat* crashed against the hideous black ship and the impact cracked her tough hull. Her spine buckled; her heat shield tore apart, and she fell from the larger vessel like a bug falling from a windshield. In the spherical Star Chamber at her heart, the virtual screens flared and died; part of the ceiling collapsed; sparks flew from crippled instrument panels and burning plastic fumes filled the air.

Sal Dervish sagged against the crash webbing in his couch. His neck hurt. With most of the external cameras gone, he was blind and disorientated; unable to tell where he was, or what state his ship was in. His only functioning screens showed empty space, distant stars.

He looked around for Dieter. Without straps to restrain him, the young man had been catapulted forward and smashed against an instrument panel. There was blood in his hair and his head lay at an awkward angle.

In the co-pilot's position, Tamara Vance lolled against her straps, unconscious. They were here because of her. Her eyes were closed, her face slack. He reached out to touch her hand and she started.

"What happened?" she said. There was blood on her chin, where she'd bitten her lip. "Did we kill it?"

Sal shook his head. "We hit it, but I don't think it noticed. It slapped us aside and kept right on going."

"And we survived?" She sounded unsure. She rubbed her forehead with the back of her hand.

He nodded. He ran his fingertips over the unresponsive instruments. His pulse was racing, hammering in his ears. There was a bubbling laugh in his throat and he had to bite down hard, afraid to let it out.

"I told you this ship was tough," he said. "How's the leg?"

"Painful." She dabbed tentatively at the blood on her chin with the sleeve of her flight suit. Her ponytail was coming loose, and untidy strands of copper-coloured hair fell around her face. Sal gave her a grin. He could see she was shaken but he couldn't help it. A burden had been lifted from him. He'd done penance for his cowardice, thrown himself into battle and emerged alive, if not triumphant.

"Did you get it all on film?" he asked.

The corner of her mouth twitched upward. She still held the recorder in her lap, although the cables connecting it to the ship's systems had been ripped loose.

"Everything up until the crash," she said.

He unbuckled and reached for Dieter's gun. He picked it up and blew dust off the barrel. It was a matt black plastic pistol. It looked ugly and vicious and expensive, and it felt great.

"What are you going to do with that?" she said.

"I don't know," he said, shrugging. He just wanted to hold it. It was a victory celebration, like a finger of defiance to the universe that had – once again – failed to kill him.

He pointed it at Dieter. "Why didn't you tell me who he was?" he said.

"Because I knew you'd never let him on board, and getting both of your reactions was too good an opportunity to pass up," Tamara said.

She swiveled around and tapped the instrument panel with distaste. The few functioning readouts showed only that the Bradley engines were offline and hemorrhaging fuel.

"So, how do we get home? We're still venting oxygen and it looks to me like the ship's pretty wrecked."

He knew he should be angry with her for lying to him, but he couldn't summon up the energy. Instead, he closed one eye and sighted the gun on Dieter's forehead. He pictured himself pulling the trigger.

"We've got an automatic distress beacon," he said.

"No-one's going to hear that before we run out of air. We're in the middle of nowhere."

He closed his eyes. His euphoria was gone and all he really wanted now was to go back to his cabin, grab a shower and get some sleep.

"The chances are slim," he admitted.

"Then what do you suggest?" she said through gritted teeth.

He scanned the room. There was an emergency locker marked with red flashes. He pulled it open and brought out a couple of lightweight pressure suits.

"We'll use these," he said. "Their air recyclers are good for days. We'll have time to think of something."

She looked down. "What about Dieter?" she said.

Sal grunted and put a hand on the back of his neck, where it still hurt. "Let's stuff him in one of the emergency sleep tanks and worry what to do with him later."

They were quiet for a moment, unwilling to look at each other. They both knew that with his injuries, there was a good chance Dieter wouldn't survive the freezing process.

Eventually, Tamara pulled herself upright and looked down at her bloody thigh. She smoothed back her hair and folded her arms.

"Screw him," she said.

Over the next few hours, the *Wild Cat* faded around them like a candle guttering. Sal didn't think she'd ever fly properly again; her back was broken, her engines wrecked. Despite the efforts of her auto-repair packages, her vital systems were failing one by one, leaking away or freezing in the darkness.

He sat there, in his control couch, with the black box resting on his knees and Dieter's pistol in a thigh pocket. The air in his suit smelled of sweat and fear. The overhead lights sparked and fluttered fitfully as the power fluctuated in the damaged reactor. And all the while, he thought of Kate.

"Tell me about her," Tamara said, in one of her lucid moments.

Sal wrinkled his nose; he didn't want to talk about her, not now, at the end.

He said, "She was just the most incredible person I ever met."

He hugged himself as best he could in the cumbersome suit. The temperature on the bridge had been falling steadily and was already well below freezing.

He began to feel light-headed and drowsy. Despite what he'd told Tamara, the air recyclers weren't designed for long duration use and probably wouldn't last much longer, certainly no more than a day.

She coughed and muttered. The painkillers had worn off and she was slipping in and out of a tormented sleep. Beneath her visor, she looked weak and pale.

"This wasn't how it was supposed to be," Sal said, aware he was talking to himself. A long, drawn-out death wasn't something he'd bargained for when he decided to ram the alien ship. He'd hoped to go out in a blaze of glory and redemption, not linger here, slowly fading. His empty stomach was an uncomfortable knot. His throat was dry. His suit itched and chafed. But somehow, none of it really mattered. What mattered was that he'd come here to make peace with the past. He'd made a decision and faced the consequences. His only regret was that Tamara had to share his fate. But then, without her cajoling, he might never have come back. He might have died alone, on Pik Station, in disgrace.

He used the functioning console to divert the last of the ship's power to the self-repair packages, hoping it might buy them a bit more time. And then he lay and looked at the ceiling. Beside him, sexless in her thick pressure suit, Tamara groaned and swore and thrashed. She was disorientated from the drugs. She clawed at her faceplate with gloved fingers until he used the medical interface on the wrist of her suit to trigger morphine into her system.

"We're going to die," she sobbed, her cries melting into the warmth of the drug. "We can't last more than a few days without water. We're both going to die."

He did his best to keep her comfortable. He thought about putting her into one of the emergency sleep tanks next to Dieter's, but couldn't summon the energy. As the hours wore away, his eyelids became heavier and heavier. His thoughts became slippery and vague. He saw Kate's face. He saw the dark muddy water of Lowell Creek. And then...

An insistent beeping in his headphones woke him. He stirred, moving stiffly. His lips felt cracked and his fingers and toes hurt because they were so cold.

Beneath a thin layer of frost, there were a handful of lights blinking on the control console. The self-repair packages had brought the Bradley engines back online.

He nudged Tamara. "Hey, we've got power," he said.

But even as he spoke, something caught his eye. On one of the remaining functional screens, something big and black moved purposefully against the stars. A proximity warning pinged on the main flight console as the ship's autopilot tagged the intruder, logging its position and vector as a possible threat.

Tamara opened her eyes. She looked awful. Her head swayed from side-to-side, weighed down by the helmet.

"We can go home?" she said.

Sal bit his lip. They could jump into hyperspace, but the heat shielding was damaged and they had no way to navigate.

"The black ship's coming back," he said.

He glanced over, but she'd closed her eyes again. He ran a quick check on her air supply and frowned at the result. She was good for a couple of hours, maybe. She had enough oxygen to make it back to Pik Station, if he could take them straight there. But he had no way to navigate. They could end up anywhere, if they didn't burn up in the process.

He felt his lips twitch in a smile.

"No air and a damaged heat shield," he said. Surely this would be the ultimate random jump – if they survived it, he'd get his reputation back, whether he wanted it or not.

He looked at the screen: The black ship was closing. It would be in striking range in six seconds.

Four seconds.

He reached out and placed his gauntleted hand on the touch screen that controlled the Bradley engines. Despite the cold, his palms were sweating.

Two seconds.

One.

His lips peeled back in a fierce grin. He pressed down on the screen and the *Wild Cat* groaned. She shook herself like a wounded animal, and leapt.

Distant Galaxies Colliding

It was a damp afternoon in November, and wet leaves blew down the narrow streets. I ordered tea at a pavement café near the Seine while I waited for Candy to arrive. When she did, she was carrying a white cane and wearing a cheap pair of plastic sunglasses. She'd been mugged by a teenage gang on the streets of Hamburg. They'd stolen her camera and sprayed paint into her eyes.

She held onto my arm as we walked south on the Boulevard Saint Michel, toward my hotel. Pigeons and scraps of newspaper flapped around our feet. Behind us, the towers of Notre Dame grazed the sagging sky.

Paris, she said, smelt of neglect; it reminded her of Dublin, or London.

"Do you want to talk about it?" I asked, meaning Hamburg.

She squeezed my arm fiercely and her cheek brushed my shoulder. For half a second, we were off balance.

"Perhaps later," she said.

I led her across the road and up the steps of my hotel. My room was on the fourth floor. When I opened the door, she dropped her cane and sat on the bed. There were a few possessions on the nightstand: my passport; a handful of coins; a magpie feather. She stirred them with her finger as I drew the curtains.

"I'm thinking of going back to the States," she said. She rolled onto her back and began toying with the feather, dabbing it lightly against her nose.

I didn't reply; I didn't want her to go. The last few weeks without her had been almost unbearable.

"There's nothing left for me here," she said.

I knelt beside her and touched the golden stubble on her scalp. It was rough, like Velcro.

"I'm here for you."

Her arm fell to the bed. She dropped the feather and turned her head away.

There was something digging into my knee. It was a small hardback book. It must have fallen from her coat pocket. I picked it up; it was a copy of her latest collection of published photographs. The dust jacket was torn.

"When will you leave?" I asked.

She shrugged. Outside on the street, a siren wailed. At the lights, the taxis idled. We could hear their turbines ticking over.

"As soon as possible," she said.

I first met Candy about a year ago, in one of those nameless bars that litter the waterfront around Canary Wharf. My divorce had just come through and I was working freelance, writing articles for an online arts magazine. Candy was an up-and-coming American photographer, and I was supposed to be interviewing her. She wore too much jewellery and always seemed to be chewing something. When we shook hands, her fingers were cool, but her eyes were restless.

"Do you want to get something to eat?" she asked. It was around seven-thirty on a wet October evening and the place was crowded. I hadn't eaten since breakfast, so we drove over to Hammersmith, where I knew a quiet Moroccan restaurant. Inside, it smelled of incense and fried onions.

She showed me some samples of her work; pictures of street children and famine victims. They were very good, very poignant, but she seemed dissatisfied with them. When the food arrived, she spat her gum into a serviette.

"So," she said, stirring the couscous on her plate, "what do you want to know?"

I leaned forward.

"Just the facts," I said.

She flashed a crooked smile. "You want to know if I'm going to go home with you tonight, don't you?"

"I guess."

She tilted her head. The cheap jeweled stud in her ear caught the candlelight. "Are you always so forward?"

We ate in silence for a while, listening to the chef rattling pans in the kitchen. I'd opted for the chicken tagine. It was flavoured with pickled lemons and olives.

"I've just come out of a bad relationship," I said.

"I know." She covered my hand with her own. "I can tell."

The traffic outside was queued back from the flyover. We finished our meal and went back to my flat.

That first night, I left the lights off and the curtains open. I made coffee by the orange streetlight and watched her undress. The rain running down the window cast eerie underwater shadows on her pale skin.

Two weeks later we flew out to Greece, then Turkey. Her work carried her all over, and I tagged along when I could.

She was always restless, always ready to move on. She lived out of a rucksack, preferring to buy things when she needed them rather than weigh herself down.

That winter, she walked through Athens and Istanbul, her digital camera clicking furiously.

"I'm a professional tourist," she said.

I remember sitting beneath a tree, beside a ruined temple, looking out at the Aegean. The water and sky were a matching blue, and the white sun burned above us. I'd been sifting through some of her downloaded images on my palmtop, but now the battery was running low.

"Do you know," she said, "that Earth is the only planet whose English name isn't derived from Greek or Roman mythology?"

I smiled. I closed the palmtop and lay back against the tree. The bark was gnarled and warm. Goats grazed among the fallen stones of the temple, and the air smelled faintly of dry grass and dung.

"What's that got to do with anything?"

She came over and sat beside me. She'd spent all morning looking

91

around the temple, recording it all. She wore a white cotton dress with big, wooden buttons up the front.

"I don't know," she said. She reached into her shoulder bag and pulled out the magazine she'd bought at the airport. There was an article in it about the old Hubble telescope; the accompanying picture showed two distant galaxies colliding.

"Look at that for a picture," she said, using a fingernail to trace the dusty whorls of tortured stars.

"It's pretty," I said.

Candy frowned. "The light from these stars is a million years old," she said. "It's been travelling through space since before the dawn of civilisation."

We looked around at the collapsed walls, the moss and lichen covering the scattered stones. They looked so much a part of the landscape that it was difficult to imagine the headland without them.

"It makes what I'm doing seem so bloody ephemeral." She pushed her blonde hair back and dropped the magazine. When she looked across at me, her eyes were the same shade of green as the sunlight filtering through the leafy branches above.

"I like your pictures," I said.

She ignored me. She rolled onto her front and put her chin on her fist.

"I could be doing so much more," she said.

Despite her doubts, the pictures she took that day were startling. She had a knack for picking out details: a flower blooming from beneath a crumbled pillar; a crushed cola can glinting in the Mediterranean sun; a vapour trail above an ancient olive grove.

Many of those pictures wound up in the collection that I now held in my hand. Kneeling beside the bed in that Parisian hotel, I flicked through the pages.

They were mostly pictures of collapsed and overgrown buildings, but there were a few pictures of the night sky, taken from various locations.

This wasn't just her latest collection of photographs, I realised sadly. It was also going to be her last.

When we'd originally arranged to meet in Paris, six weeks ago, she'd been hoping to visit the ESA headquarters. She'd wanted to use a deep range telescope for her next project. She'd wanted to find a way to make art out of science, to express how small and insignificant the universe made her feel.

Now, she wouldn't have the chance.

She'd never take another picture; there'd never be another collection. She'd have to find another way to express herself.

She heard the rustle of glossy pages and her head turned toward the sound. Behind her sunglasses, I could see the white gauze dressings that covered her eyes.

"What are you reading?" she asked.

I lied; I said it was a guidebook.

She held a hand out to me. Her fingers were cold and dry.

"Open the curtains," she whispered, "and tell me what you see."

I pulled myself up and pocketed the book.

"Why?"

She turned away and hugged the pillow to her chest. Her knees were drawn up and her feet were tangled in her skirt.

"Because I want my final image of Europe to be a good one," she said.

She looked so frail and vulnerable, I couldn't refuse her. I stepped over to the window, pulled back the curtain, and began to describe the buildings across the street.

Candy, fumbling on the bedside table, managed to switch on the clock radio; gentle Cuban music filled the room, like cigarette smoke. A light rain began to fall. It was getting dark and the orange streetlights painted everything with their false colours, reminding me of our first night in Hammersmith, twelve short months before.

As I spoke, I thought of those kids in Hamburg, of what they'd done. Had they simply been trying to steal her camera, or did they blind her because they were jealous of the things she'd seen? In their vicious and brutal way, they'd taken far more from her than simply her sight, and I doubted if she'd ever fully recover.

"Can you see the stars?" she asked.

I said no.

A woman appeared below, framed in a café doorway. She lit a cigarette and turned up the collar of her raincoat. As she hurried up the street, the wet leaves snagged on her high heels. At the corner, she stopped to scratch her leg, where the impurities of her ankle chain had irritated the skin.

I told Candy that it would have made a perfect picture. I felt her move up behind me. Her hands touched my shoulders.

"I guess that'll have to do, then," she said.

Falling Apart

When the train from London Paddington arrived in Weston Super Mare, Kadie Jones stepped off with a briefcase full of money and eight morphine syringes. Her heavy boots crunched on the icy platform. She hadn't slept for thirty-six hours; she was tired and train-lagged and all she wanted was a hot bath and a stiff drink; but she couldn't afford to relax just yet.

Outside the station, she found a couple of taxis idling at a rank. She walked over and climbed into the nearest. It was an old Honda, retrofitted with an alcohol engine.

"Where to, love?" said the driver. He was little more than a hunched silhouette in the darkness.

"Do you know the Grove Hotel?"

There was a lurch and the car began to roll forward, coughing fumes.

The driver said, "I don't get much call to take people up there, these days."

Kadie pulled the fake fur hat from her head and ran a gloved hand through her mussed hair.

"No," she said, "I don't suppose you do."

They passed along the sea front. Weston had become a desolate, half-forgotten place. Most of the shops and amusement arcades were boarded-up. The sun had set out beyond the mouth of the estuary and the wind had dropped, leaving the muddy water like a sheet of glass in the last cold light of the dying day.

At the end of the promenade, they headed uphill and the taxi stopped in the road.

"Here we are."

The hotel was a four-storey Victorian building with brittle brown wisps of ivy on its discoloured stonework. Kadie fastened her long coat, paid the driver and hefted her case up the icy steps and into the reception foyer.

Behind the counter, an old woman squinted at a well-thumbed newspaper. She looked up as Kadie stamped snow from her boots.

"Can I help you, love?" she said.

"I'm here to see one of your guests, Vincent Jones."

The woman glanced down at her briefcase.

"Doctor, are you?"

Kadie shook her head. "I'm his ex-wife."

The woman's eyes narrowed and she nodded toward a door near the elevator.

"He's in the bar," she said.

She found Vince sitting alone at a table by the window. He'd lost a lot of weight and his skin looked grey and waxy.

"I got your email," she said.

Above a shaky Marlboro, his eyes burned with desperation.

"Did you bring them?"

She reached into her coat pocket and pulled out the syringes. "Do you mean these?" she said.

He snatched them up with both hands and stuffed them into the folds of his threadbare cardigan.

"Thank you," he said.

On the table were two glasses and a bottle of cheap wholesale gin. Kadie picked up the unused glass, wiped the rim on the hem of her coat, and filled it.

"How's the pain?" she asked.

Vince grunted. "It's bad enough."

He ground out the butt of his cigarette in the plastic ashtray and, after a moment's indecision, lit another.

"How was London?"

Kadie looked around at the smoke-stained pictures on the walls, the fading drapes and crooked sash windows. Somewhere above, pipes clanked as an unseen guest drew a bath.

"It was scary," she said. "People are frightened; everyone's jumpy."

"I heard there were riots."

She took a sip. "The government had to put troops on the street; I was lucky to get out."

"Have you been back to Glasgow recently?"

"Not for a long time."

The gin tasted like nail polish but she could feel its warmth spreading down through her chest. She shrugged off her coat and stuffed her gloves into the pockets.

"You look tired," he said.

She pushed her hair back. "I haven't slept much since you called me."

"I know what you mean." He took the bottle and splashed another measure into his glass. "I haven't slept since the doctor told me about the, you know." He gestured vaguely at his stomach. He took a long drag on the Marlboro and Kadie could see the white of his cheekbones where they stretched the papery skin. She reached out and took his hand. Somehow it felt too light and dry, like an old stick.

"I know why you want all that morphine," she said.

He looked away. "You figured that out, did you?"

She let go of his fingers. "It wasn't hard."

He looked at her, his expression brittle. "And I suppose you're going to try and talk me out of it?"

She nodded.

"But first," she patted the briefcase by her foot, "There's something I need to show you."

To get some privacy, he took her back to his room. Inside, it smelt of sickness and disinfectant. Discarded clothes and old newspapers covered the bed; dirty plates and empty bottles littered the floor.

Kadie crossed to the dressing table and opened the case, revealing the stacked bundles of high denomination banknotes within.

Vince's eyes widened in surprise.

"I've been putting it aside for a rainy day," she said.

He reached out skeletal fingers to brush the edge of the case. "How much is there?"

"A hundred and forty thousand, give or take."

"That's a lot of money."

She snapped the case shut. "It's enough."

He sat on the edge of the duvet and lit another cigarette. "Enough for what?" he said.

She crossed the room and perched on the bed beside him. Beneath her hand, his shoulder felt bony and unfamiliar.

"I want you to come with me," she said.

"Where?"

She reached into her back pocket and pulled out a creased brochure. On the cover was a picture of the Magellan. She was a residential cruise ship, a permanent floating refuge for the super-rich.

"They have some of the best medical facilities in the world. They'll be able to help you," she said.

The ship was moored off Cardiff, taking on supplies. If they could bribe their way aboard, there was a chance she could use the remaining money to buy him some treatment.

He shook his head. "It's too late," he said.

"No it isn't," she said, springing to her feet and pacing over to the briefcase. "And even if it is, wouldn't you prefer to spend your last hours in comfort, rather than fading away in some forgotten, dingy hotel?"

Vince reached into his cardigan and pulled out one of the morphine syringes.

His voice cracked as he said, "So why did you bring me these?"

She took a deep breath. "Because I wanted to give you a choice," she said. "Now, are you going to help me or not?"

"Help you?" Vince swept his arm around in a gesture that took in the stained sink, the untidy bed and the bottles of painkillers on the dresser. "What can I do?"

Kadie bent forward and looked him in the eye.

"You can find us a boat," she said.

The Kings Head had once been a restaurant. Now, it was a drinking den for the local fishermen; from the front door, you could see their boats moored in the shadow of the Old Pier.

"Do you think we'll find someone in here?" Kadie whispered,

looking around the crowded booths. Beside her, wrapped in a long black leather coat and thick woollen scarf, Vince nodded.

"There's a lot of drugs and immigrants that come through here from the continent," he said. "Not to mention cheap fags and booze."

They crossed to the bar and she let him order a couple of pints of the local beer. When it came, it was cloudy and sweet.

He lit a Marlboro and closed his eyes. In the dim light, with the black coat, he looked like a Gestapo officer. She tried to remember him as he'd been before the illness: energetic and enthusiastic, ready to take on the world. They'd had their share of rough times, especially after the divorce, but now, with his illness and everything, none of that seemed to matter.

"Are you okay?" she said. She could see he'd rather be somewhere else.

He opened his eyes. "I'll be fine."

In the far corner, there was a plasma screen tuned to a rolling news channel. She saw pictures of riots and burning cars, floods and crashing stock markets. When it showed clips of starving children in the Far East, she looked away.

Vince leaned toward her. He pointed out a figure slumped on a stool at the end of the bar.

"If you really want to do this, then that's your man," he said. "They call him McGuire. He does a lot of business with the cruise ships."

"Really? How do you know?" she said. Her gaze flicked from the man's thick, shapeless jersey and patchy beard to the tattoos on his forearms.

Vince dropped the end of his cigarette and ground it out with his toe.

Without looking up, he said, "I've been smoking a lot of marijuana recently, for the pain. McGuire brings it in on his boat."

The big man led them out to the narrow, poorly lit car park behind the pub, where they could talk without being overheard.

"What can I do you for?" he said. His voice was rough, with a thick West Country accent.

"We need a ride to the *Magellan*," Vince said.

McGuire looked him up and down, and then shook his head. "You'd never get past their security."

"Could you?" Kadie asked.

McGuire smiled. "Yes, love. But they turn a blind eye to me because I'm only making deliveries. I don't think you could afford what it would cost me to get you aboard."

"We have money," Vince said.

McGuire scratched the back of his tattooed neck and glanced off, down the street. "You're talking false papers, bribes – I'd need at least seventy-five thousand."

Kadie tapped the side of her case meaningfully.

He raised an eyebrow. "Really?"

She moved the case away. "Don't try anything," she warned. Her breath was like a silver cloud in the freezing night air.

McGuire glanced at the two of them, transparently weighing his chances. Then he pulled a serrated fishing knife from his belt.

He said, "How about you just hand that money to me?"

Kadie took a step back, placing the case on the ground behind her. "How about you come and get it?" she said.

In her peripheral vision she could see Vince tensing, his fists clenched. She waved him away.

McGuire snorted. "I'm not afraid to cut a woman," he said.

Kadie locked her fingers together and pushed her arms out until her knuckles crackled.

"You should be."

She waited for him to come to her. He was big and powerful but he moved awkwardly, not like a serious street fighter. Not like the kind of people she'd had to deal with in London. When he finally got close enough to take a swipe at her, she grabbed his wrist and twisted the knife out of his hand. He yelled in pain. He grabbed at her but a hard knee to the groin sent him sprawling on the cold ground, where he lay curled around the pain, legs squeezed together and feet writhing in the snow.

She bent down and slipped the knife into her pocket.

Vince stepped forward, mouth open.

"I've never seen you move like that," he said.

She shrugged. "I've had to learn a lot in the last couple of years."

She grabbed McGuire by the lapels and dragged him to his feet.

"Now," she said, "are you going to co-operate?"

*

He led them down to the muddy water and onto a floating jetty. The wooden planks were slippery and the whole thing wallowed gently as they walked on it. It smelled of salt water and sticky river mud. His boat was an old trawler, moored at the end. As they drew near, Vince hung back. He looked over his shoulder at the lights of the promenade.

"I don't know about this," he said, and coughed.

A thin, bitter wind blew in off the Estuary. Down the coast, chunks of sea ice bobbed on the swell like pale ghosts. Kadie pulled her fur hat down, over her ears.

"You don't know about what?" she said.

"All this." He swept an arm at the boat and the water beyond. "I can't help thinking it's futile."

She took him by the shoulder. "Don't you dare do this," she said. "Not now."

He squirmed in her grip. He was lighter and weaker than she remembered.

"I haven't got long," he said. "It could be a matter of weeks, or days."

She let go. "I don't care. I'm not going to leave you here."

"It might be for the best. I have the morphine. I could use it, all at once."

He took a deep breath. She wanted to slap him but he looked so fragile and ill that she pulled him close and kissed him instead.

"Just because everything else is falling apart," she said, "it doesn't mean we have to."

He looked into her eyes. She could see he wanted to believe her.

"But everything that's happened between us..." he said.

Kadie stopped him with a wave of her hand. She said, "Forget it. All that matters is that we're here, now, together."

McGuire started the trawler's engine and it coughed out a cloud of diesel exhaust. She put an arm under Vince's shoulder. He tried to speak but couldn't. He coughed into his fist.

"I'm not leaving without you," she said.

As they cut through the still surface of the Estuary, she sat in the stern and watched the lights of the town fade behind them. Above, a handful of stars were visible between the low snow clouds. To the East, the sky was beginning to turn grey with the first light of a cold dawn. Music drifted from a radio in the wheelhouse, accompanied by the thick smell of smuggled marijuana. Since their scuffle, McGuire hadn't given her any more trouble. In fact, he'd hardly spoken and he wouldn't look her in the eye.

She glanced at her watch. It was going to take another two hours to catch up with the *Magellan* on the other side of the estuary.

Across the water, on the Welsh coast, houses were burning.

"You'd think the government would be able to do something," she said.

Vince pulled a fresh pack of counterfeit Marlboro from his coat pocket and lit up.

"There's nothing they can do," he said.

Kadie looked down at the water foaming in their spreading wake. She said, "So this is the way the world ends, with everything collapsing?"

Vince flicked his cigarette overboard. They watched its spinning red spark fall into the water.

"I'm afraid so," he said, shaking his head.

They sat in silence for a while, rocked by the motion of the boat. To the East, the sky continued to brighten.

"Still, we've got the money," Kadie said at length.

In the wheelhouse, McGuire began to sing along with the music, his voice low and husky, and hopelessly out of tune.

Vince smiled. "Yes," he said. "We've got the money."

Kadie reached for his hand and squeezed it gently. "And we've got each other."

"Yes."

She bit her lip. "So, let's make the most of it."

"How do you mean?"

She shifted closer and rested her head on his shoulder.

"Neither of us is going to die today, right?"

"I suppose."

She slid an arm around his waist and closed her eyes as the boat rocked. She could smell the leather of his coat. She turned her head and kissed his neck.

"Then let's just take each day as it comes," she said.

Morning Star

Nick Malik paused outside Huczynski's tattoo parlour, looking up. Overhead, dirty Martian snow fell like pinkish static against the transparent walls of the pressurized city dome, and the streets around him held their breath, caught in the twilight lull, suspended between the cold of late afternoon and the bitterness of early evening.

He'd spent his last few credits on a cup of coffee from a roadside stall and it had temporarily taken away his fatigue, and dulled the hunger that usually kept his stomach clenched around itself like a fist. For the first time in days he felt relaxed and clear-headed, ready for his weekly confrontation with Huczynski.

As he pushed open the tattoo parlour door, the clock icon in his left eye read six forty-five, local time. He caught sight of his reflection in the glass – unshaven, pale and thin. Huczynski paid him good money, but not enough to live on.

Huczynski was a short woman with hair and fingernails the rusty colour of dried blood. He found her standing behind the desk in the back room office, a silver travel case sitting at her feet like an attendant familiar.

"You're late," she said.

Malik shrugged. "I had to see Spicer – he had a delivery for me."

"I don't care about that. Have you got the files?"

"Most of them."

Huczynski reached into a drawer and pulled out the uplink. She seemed unusually agitated.

"We don't have much time," she said.

She pressed the thumb-sized uplink to his temple, downloading the files stored in his neural implant – the same files he'd scanned earlier that afternoon from Pia's computer terminal.

When it was done, she pocketed the uplink, then bent at the knees and picked up the silver case.

"Are you going somewhere?" he said.

She straightened up, leaning slightly to compensate for the case's weight.

"We've had word from Bullock. We're pulling out – and I suggest you do the same."

"Have we been compromised?"

Huczynski nodded. Bullock was her boss, a shadowy figure in Tanguy's management structure.

She said, "That money I gave you last time? Don't try to buy anything with it."

"Why not?"

"We got ripped off. It's all forged, and forged badly at that. Last night, Larsson Security picked up one of our contacts trying to spend some of it in a bar."

"Do you think he'll talk?" Malik said.

Huczynski's smile was bleak. She said, "Everyone talks, sooner or later."

She hefted the case, as if about to leave, and then paused.

"That's not the only reason we're going, though," she said.

"There's something else?"

She raked her hair back. "I shouldn't be telling you this but last night Tanguy troops attacked a Larsson prospecting expedition in the northern desert."

Malik shrugged. Skirmishes between the mega corporations were common, certainly no cause for alarm.

"Has Larsson retaliated?" he asked.

"Not yet." Huczynski checked her wristwatch. "But I got a warning from Bullock about an hour ago. He's decoded one of the reports you stole from that lab assistant you're sleeping with."

"Her name's Pia."

"Whatever." Huczynski took a step toward the door and shifted the case from one hand to the other. "It seems they're planning to test one of their biological weapons against us," she said.

"Against Tanguy, you mean?"

"They're going to hit our offices in Anaheim at midnight tonight." Malik's mouth felt dry. There were eighteen thousand people in Anaheim.

"Isn't there anything we can do?"

Huczynski leaned toward him, her voice lowered. "Bullock's got it all figured out. At nine o'clock, the guidance systems on one of our automated cargo shuttles, the *Morning Star*, will fail during re-entry. It'll hit Roxport at nine-oh-five, destroying the lab facility before they can deploy the weapon."

She straightened up and brushed an imaginary speck of dirt from her jacket with rust-coloured nails. "So I suggest you get out."

Malik nodded, stunned. The *Morning Star* would hit the town like a bomb, vapourising the lab and large areas of downtown. And with the dome breached, the only survivors would be those lucky enough to find themselves in pressurised buildings or shelters at the moment of impact. Huczynski was watching him closely, and he sensed a concern that she'd never shown before.

"Are you okay?" she asked.

He nodded. "I will be."

She checked her watch again. "I shouldn't have told you any of that, but you deserve a chance to escape. You've got a little under two hours. Go home, grab what you need, and get to the station. But be careful – if you get arrested, that's it, game over."

She opened the office door and he followed her through the darkened tattoo parlour. Outside, rickshaws drifted along the street. Music came from the open doorways of the bars and cafés and cybersex joints. From the edge of town came the rumble of a departing spaceplane.

Roxport was a company town, constructed and operated by Larsson Industries as a scientific outpost and ore refinery. The streets were narrow and the buildings varied from the glass-fronted offices and fashionable ziggurat apartment blocks surrounding the decorative downtown plazas, to the huddled pressure bubbles and prefab shelters of the Fringe, the shantytown that clung lichen-like to the edge of the dome. The inhabitants of the Fringe were the flotsam of the colonisation effort: dealers, drifters and artists, bankrupt settlers and failed pioneers – an underclass of the unemployed and the unemployable, trapped on the edge of Roxport because they couldn't scrape together enough money for a ticket back to Earth.

It was where Huczynski had found him, two years ago.

They paused for a moment, their breath clouding in the night air, and he noticed she hadn't bothered to lock the tattoo parlour door.

"I've got a train to catch," she said, waving to a cab that idled outside a Sushi bar a few doors down.

Malik nodded and she squeezed his upper arm with an unexpected tenderness.

"Good luck," she said.

Pia Licari was asleep on the couch as he let himself into her apartment. The only illumination came from the bars of orange street lighting that slanted through the slats of the window blind. A few loose strands of hair trailed across her face. Her skin was pale and there were dark rings under her eyes. He crossed to the refrigerator and took out a beer. As he cracked the seal, he heard her stir.

"Nick? Is that you?" she said. She propped herself up on one elbow and rubbed her eyes with forefinger and thumb. "What time is it?"

"About seven-fifteen," he said.

"What are you doing?"

"I'm having a drink." He waggled the bottle. "Do you want one?"

She sat upright and clicked her fingers. The lights in the apartment came up slowly.

"Did you see Spicer?" she said. "Did he have it?"

Malik pulled a spray-hypo of Rhapsody from his jacket pocket. "Do you mean this?" he said.

She held a hand out for it. She looked tired and irritable.

"Don't start," she said, "I've had a bad day."

"It's going to get a whole lot worse, real soon."

"What do you mean?"

He tossed her the hypo. "Take that first, and then I'll tell you."

*

He had to look away as she injected herself. Her addiction had left its mark on her forearm, where tiny circular bruises from previous injections dappled the skin like malignant yellow freckles.

Rhapsody was a military spin-off – highly illegal and highly addictive. Taken in large enough doses, it produced a zombie-like state of emotional calm. And Malik had encouraged Pia's dependence on it in the name of industrial espionage. Somewhere deep inside, he knew he'd carry the shame of that for the rest of his life.

He drained his beer bulb and waited until she collapsed back onto the couch – then he moved over to the terminal in the corner. There was one last thing that he had to do.

For the last two months, he'd been using her terminal to access files from the weapons lab. It had been a slow and frustrating process, sifting through the server week after week, slowly copying coded files to his implant. But now – with the coming city-wide destruction – there was no need for that sort of subtlety.

He used Pia's password to access the lab's database, and then he turned his implant to maximum scan. This time, there'd be no sneaking around. This time he wanted it all, every scrap of information on the weapons they were developing. If he got out of Roxport before the crash, he'd be penniless – but if he had something valuable to sell, something the other multinationals would pay for... This data could be their passport to a better life.

The download seemed to take forever, and he began to sweat. As soon as it finished, he turned back to Pia and kicked the couch by her feet.

"C'mon, get up," he said.

"What's the matter?" She squinted up at him, rubbing a bleary eye with the heel of her hand.

"We're leaving," he said.

"Why?"

"Because we've only got an hour and forty minutes left before all hell breaks loose."

She sat up, her face calm with the soothing smoothness of the Rhapsody.

"What do you mean?" she said.

"There's going to be a shuttle crash." He mimed an explosion with his hands. "And the dome's going to get punctured."

She tilted her head to one side. "What?"

He pushed a hand back through his lank hair. "Just trust me."

He crossed to the wardrobe and stuffed a few random handfuls of her clothes into a holdall.

"You're serious, aren't you?" she said, following him.

"Yes," he said. "And you're just stoned enough to deal with it in a calm and rational manner."

He threw the bag at her and blinked up a net display in his left eye. A few sub vocal commands took him to the train schedule. There was a departure for Anaheim due in thirty minutes. He booked two tickets and flagged an automatic request for a cab to pick them up from outside the apartment.

"Is this something to do with the bio-weapon test tonight?" Pia said.

Malik nodded. "The people you're targeting aren't too keen to find out how effective it is."

"What people?" She climbed stiffly to her feet.

Malik didn't bother to reply, crossing instead to the window, where he looked through the blind into the street below. He didn't know how quickly Larsson Security would react to his crashing around in the lab's database, but he hoped he'd have time to get to the station before anyone came knocking. He could feel his heart thumping in his chest. With a shaky hand, he patted his jacket pocket, where he carried a second hypo of Rhapsody. Pia was cool at the moment but it paid to have a back up. If they were delayed, he didn't want her going through a crash detox on the train and drawing unwelcome attention.

"Who do you work for?" she said.

"What?"

"I'm serious, Nick."

He shook his head and picked up the discarded hypo-spray. "What do you care, as long as I keep bringing you these?"

He tossed it to her and she caught it by reflex, then dropped it and stepped back as if stung.

"That's not fair," she said. Her tone was flat, matter-of-fact, where he'd expected anger. He turned away so she wouldn't see his guilt.

"It's up to you," he said roughly. "Stay here and die, or come with me – now."

*

They arrived at the station just in time to see a handcuffed Huczynski being pushed into the back of a Security rover. Armed troops blocked every exit, scanning everyone stepping on to the platform. Malik hunched down and told the driver to keep going. If they knew who Huczynski was, the chances were they'd be looking for him too.

As they drove, the passing shop fronts and overhanging balconies, the plazas and markets, slid by the cab window like grainy newsreel footage, a backdrop for the early evening citizens hurrying along the cold pavements in their thick jackets, unaware of the impending attack. For a mad instant he wanted to throw open the car door and warn them, give them a chance to escape, as Huczynski had done for him. But he knew he couldn't.

It's just numbers, he kept telling himself – cold, hard numbers. Nine thousand people would die when the shuttle hit Roxport. But as a result, eighteen thousand people in Anaheim would be spared. For their sake he had to keep quiet, to make sure the weapons lab was destroyed.

Beside him, Pia hugged her holdall to her chest.

"So how are we going to get out?" she said.

He closed his eyes. How indeed? With the station closed, they were trapped.

"Have you got any money?" he asked, thinking they could maybe bribe their way past the soldiers.

She shook her head. "A few dollars, that's all. I don't get paid until the end of the month."

He swore under his breath. All he had was the counterfeit cash Huczynski had warned him about. He saw a Security rover parked on a street corner and slid further down into his seat.

Suppose they did get out before the *Morning Star* hit, what then? If they made it to Anaheim, once Tanguy's biotech division – and Bullock – got their hands on Pia, he might never see her again. He couldn't do that to her, not after everything he'd inflicted on her in the last few months – not after the Rhapsody.

He didn't want to leave her to die, and he didn't want to deliver her to his employers. There had to be an alternative.

In his left eye, the merciless countdown continued.

*

"So, you're back already?" Spicer said, pushing himself back in his chair and reaching into his leather waistcoat to scratch the red puckered skin around the symbiotech weapon jacks sunk into his chest. He was at his usual table in the dim Turkish café, drinking thick black coffee and smoking a sickly cigar. On the counter, a radio chattered in Arabic.

"What do you need?" he said. "And don't tell me more Rhapsody, 'cause there's no way you already got through what I sold you this afternoon."

Rumour had it Spicer had once been a UN marine and had acquired the fungal scarring on his face during police action in the jungles of South America. He was reputed to have contacts at all levels of Roxport society, and the word was he could fix you up with anything you needed.

Malik shook his head and said, "I need something else."

"Well then," Spicer spread his tattooed hands, "I'm open for business."

Malik pulled up a chair and leant forward across the table.

"Do you have access to the entry codes for the Larsson personnel system?" he said.

Spicer regarded him with hooded, calculating eyes as he took a mouthful of sweet smoke. The scarring on his face seemed to glow in the gloom, lit by the burning cigar.

"Need a new identity, huh?"

Malik nodded. "For myself and one other."

"Licari?"

"I figure I owe her that much."

Spicer smiled. "It'll cost you," he said.

Malik reached into his jacket pocket and pulled out a couple of counterfeit credit disks. "No problem," he said.

Spicer's hand whipped out and swept the disks from the table in one fluid movement.

"You need them right away?" he said.

Malik was sweating. He swallowed hard and tried to relax but the smell of Spicer's cigar on an empty stomach was making him feel ill.

"Travel papers, too," he said.

"Travel papers?" Spicer raised an eyebrow. "That's going to be difficult. Maybe you haven't heard, but the station's closed to all non-essential personnel. Some sort of Security operation."

Malik slipped another couple of disks onto the cracked plastic tabletop.

"I was hoping you might know of another way out," he said.

Spicer pocketed the money and fingered his commcard. It was a custom job, its smooth sides interrupted by the organic clumsiness of solder and a parasitic cluster of added components. He activated an old-fashioned virtual keyboard and tapped away for a few minutes. Malik sat back and tried to listen to the radio – it sounded like a news bulletin, but he didn't know enough Arabic to follow it.

After a while, Spicer looked up from the card with a final nod of satisfaction.

"There you go," he said.

Malik sat up straight. In the corner of his eye the readout stood at forty-five minutes and counting.

"You've got us a way out?"

"Yeah." Spicer's smile was cold. "But it's going to cost you extra."

"How much extra?"

"Four hundred."

Malik puffed his cheeks and exhaled, trying to look reluctant. He had over a thousand dollars worth of the fake disks in his pocket, but he didn't want to seem too eager to pay up in case Spicer started asking awkward questions.

"Three fifty?" he said.

"What the hell are you talking about?" Spicer said. "The price is four hundred. And it's a one time offer."

Malik slid the extra disks across and Spicer responded by passing over his commcard.

"As the station's closed, I've booked you onto a flight," he said.

"What flight?"

"Does it matter? It's all there. Scan it and get lost."

The false papers got them through the Security cordon and into the shuttle port, but Malik's surge of relief was premature and short-lived. When they reached the departure lounge they found their flight had been delayed.

"Some sort of security crisis," said the desk clerk, shrugging.

Malik felt the strength drain out of him. He led Pia over to a plastic bench, feeling numb. They'd tried every way out of the city that he could think of, and now there wasn't time to look for another. There were only twenty minutes left – they weren't going to make it.

He fished the second hypo from his coat pocket and looked at it for a long moment. And then, trying not to think, he set it for a half dose and pressed it to his thigh. He pulled the trigger and settled back on the bench, feeling nauseous.

In the end, it was Pia who got him to his feet, who dragged him to the gate when their flight was called. Lost in despair, he hadn't heard the announcement.

"What are you doing?" he protested, pulling back. Thanks to the delay, their shuttle was due to lift only seconds before the *Morning Star* struck. It was too close – at least here, in the pressurised terminal building, they might stand a chance.

She squeezed his hand, her nails digging into his knuckles. The pain shocked him. Through the detachment of the drug he saw her clearly, as if for the first time. He saw she was on the downward leg of her Rhapsody cycle. Her eyes were raw slits and she was fighting to stay awake.

"Returning a favour," she said, giving him a shove.

Beside him in the shuttle's cabin, her head lolled against the safety straps of her couch. The final effort had exhausted her. When she woke, she'd be queasy and depressed. If they made it into orbit, he'd have to try and pass it off as travel sickness, a reaction to being weightless for the first time.

In his eye, the countdown reached three minutes. Looking out of the window, he could see that they'd reached the end of the runway and were waiting on launch clearance. He checked his own straps for the hundredth time and realised that, even with the half dose of Rhapsody, his hands had begun to shake. Why was it taking so long? Surely they couldn't fail now, not after coming so far?

He tried not to think about how many people were about to be killed. The numbers were too big, too abstract. The important thing was that he was getting Pia out. She was his redemption. Whatever he'd done to her in the past, he hadn't left her there to die.

He glanced down at the names printed on the tags fixed to the breast pockets of their flight suits: Mr. and Mrs. Jack and Wanda Harvey.

"I guess we're married now," he said, using his thumb to wipe the drool from her chin. "Who would've figured Spicer as a minister?"

When they reached orbit, they'd join two hundred other technicians bound for the Larsson mining facility on Io. Their relationship so far had been built on manipulation, addiction and lies, but perhaps they could use this chance to salvage something from the wreckage, to build a new life, on a new world?

He brushed a stray hair from her face. Across the aisle, a woman with a complexion like fine marble smiled encouragingly at him.

"Is this your first flight?" she said.

He returned the smile over gritted teeth. "And last," he said.

Despite the effects of the drug, his heart was racing. There were now only two minutes left. The *Morning Star* was already on its way, streaking toward them like a fireball.

He reached out for Pia's hand. He closed his eyes, but he couldn't block out the countdown.

At one minute thirty, the noise from the engines rose to a deafening shriek and they began to roll forward. Then the thrust kicked in and pushed him back into his seat as they leapt up into the thin, cold air.

As they rose, he pushed his face to the cold window, waiting for the explosion. But by the time the countdown in his eye reached zero, they were into the dark snow clouds – and then through, with nothing but stars above.

The Last Reef

A Necklace of Ivy

We woke to grey skies and rain on the window. We knew we were going to have to cut our holiday short, so we got dressed and drove down to the sea for a last look. We had our suitcases on the back seat of the car, and it was raining as we pulled into the car park above the beach. Wet pebbles clicked and scattered beneath our wheels.

"Come on," Debs said. She opened the door and ran over to the slippery concrete steps that led down to the beach. Her thin summer dress streamed and flapped around her legs as she ran.

I pulled my coat on and followed her. But by the time I reached the foot of the steps, she was already down by the waterline, shoes in hand. As I watched, she stepped out of her clothes and waded into the waves.

"We don't have time for this," I called.

She ignored me and slid out into deeper water. For a moment, I lost her in the surf, and then saw her bob up between the waves, spluttering and laughing. She pushed her wet hair back, and the water glistened on her skin.

"Come in," she called. Then she turned and struck out parallel to the beach, swimming with strong, graceful strokes. I leaned against a rock and watched her for a few minutes. Then I started walking back toward the car. The rain made little pockmarks in the wet sand. When I reached the wooden steps, I called to her.

She came splashing out of the shallows.

"Where's my dress?" she said, looking around for it.

It lay on the sand, where it had been dropped; the water tugged at it.

"Forget it, it's wet," I said. I slipped my coat around her shoulders and she laughed.

"You're such a gentleman."

We climbed up to the car. I could smell the salt in her hair.

"That was wonderful," she said, shivering.

I unlocked the doors and slid in behind the steering wheel. She stretched out on the passenger seat. The windows started to mist, so I put the heater on.

"We'd better get going," I said.

She wrinkled her nose. "Do we have to? Can't we go somewhere else?"

I shook my head. "The bombing starts in an hour. And besides, you've only got a coat on – where were you thinking of going?"

We followed the A3083 for a few miles, occasionally passing convoys of armoured vehicles heading south. While I drove, Debs leaned back and brought her sandy feet up to rest on the dashboard. The coat fell open, showing off her slender legs.

"Are we out of cigarettes?" she said, checking the coat's pockets.

"I'm afraid so."

Where we were going – into the overcrowded refugee camps of Bristol and Bath – little luxuries like tobacco, alcohol, or toilet tissue were going to be worth their weight in gold.

"Maybe it's time we gave up," I said.

She patted my leg.

"It'll do us good." she said.

The road passed through a deserted village and dropped into a shallow valley. I downshifted for the winding climb back out.

Debs was still stretched on the seat. She turned to look out the side window, and I admired the way the tendons in her neck moved smoothly beneath the skin.

"We just need to learn to relax," she said.

We'd been in Cornwall for six days, spending time away from the city, somewhere her father couldn't find us.

We'd been staying in the spare room of a cottage owned by a friend of mine called Phil. He was a technician on one of the large antenna dishes at the Goonhilly receiving station.

We were there in his kitchen the night he came home raving about the anomalous satellite signal they'd picked up, the one that caused strange effects in the soil around the giant dish. And we were there the next morning – a Sunday – when they called him in to work, when they first started using words like 'quarantine' and 'sensible precautions'.

Two days later, the army started evacuating the surrounding villages.

"Is this something to do with that monkey that ate the Internet?" Debs asked.

Phil shook his head. "No, this is something new."

We were passing between ploughed fields, heading north on the Falmouth road.

"Can we stop somewhere?" Debs asked.

I looked at the clock on the dash. "We don't have time. We're supposed to be out of here already; we're really pushing it."

She reached out and touched my cheek. "*Please?*"

I pulled the car off the road, into the shelter of an unruly hedgerow.

When I turned off the engine, I could hear the sound of helicopters somewhere off to the west. The road was empty.

Debs refastened the coat and got out. She took my arm and led me over to a five-bar gate that opened into a ploughed field.

"There's a wood over there," she said, pointing across the field, and I sighed, already knowing what would happen.

She squeezed my arm. "You don't need to sound so resigned," she said.

I helped her across the field. The thick, sticky mud made walking difficult.

"You should take your shoes off," she said, "or you'll ruin them."

When we reached the trees, she let go of my arm. She skipped ahead, humming a bright, disjointed tune, hopping and prancing with her bare feet like a ballerina.

I looked at my watch and cursed her. We should have been long gone by now; if an army patrol pulled us up, we could be arrested, or shot.

I glanced back at the car, and Debs danced off, into the trees. I could hear her somewhere nearby, crashing and stumbling around in the undergrowth, but the rain deadened the sound and I couldn't tell for sure where she was.

I hesitated.

"Where are you?" I said.

Above, disturbed crows flapped into flight with hoarse, protesting cries.

I heard a giggle, a snapped twig, and I swore under my breath. I was annoyed and uncomfortable without my coat, and in no mood for one of her games. My shirt was wet and the cold air seemed to cut right through it; my feet were balls of mud.

"Where are you?" I asked again.

She laughed, but didn't reply.

Angry, I waded into the undergrowth, swinging a damp stick to beat down the nettles. Brambles clawed at my trousers. I blundered forward a short way, and then leaned against a gnarled tree. The rain smacked against the higher branches and dripped and trickled down to the mossy floor.

"I'm going to count to ten," I said, "and then I'm leaving."

There was another giggle, and I caught a glimpse of colour through the bushes to my right. I pushed forward and found my coat hanging from a low branch. I took it down and fished my mobile from the pocket. Its solid plastic casing gave me some reassurance. I unlocked the keypad and checked my messages. There were two – one from my editor and the other from my ex-wife. They were both worried. We were still in the quarantine zone; more villages were being evacuated, and they wanted to know if we were all right. I thought of calling them, but couldn't get a decent signal.

Debs's mirrored sunglasses were in the other pocket.

"You'd better come out," I said.

There was a rustle of leaves off to my right. She said, "I don't want to go into one of those dreadful camps, I want to stay here."

She came out from behind a bush. She wore a string of ivy around her neck. Her arms were folded and her hair plastered to her scalp.

"You'll get pneumonia," I said.

"I don't care."

She sat down and put her chin on her fist. Black dirt and wet leaves stuck to her skinny thighs. Her feet were still caked from the field.

"I want to stay here," she said. She wrapped a finger in the ivy hanging around her neck. I walked over and covered her shoulders with the coat.

"We can't. You know there's something happening. We've got to get out."

From the southwest came a series of dull, rolling thuds. She shivered again.

"Listen," I said. "They've started bombing Goonhilly."

She pulled me deeper into the trees.

Eventually, we came to a lake near the far edge of the wood. The water was a dark, vegetable green. The rain had eased into a clinging drizzle. She put her bare arms around my waist. I could feel the heat of her through my shirt.

"Let's swim," she said.

I pulled away. "Aren't you wet enough already?"

She laughed, and reached up to touch my face.

"You should try it."

She handed me the coat and put her hands on her hips.

"You know, you used to find this kind of thing exciting," she said.

I looked into the still, dark water. Overhead, jets roared through the low clouds.

I thought about her father. I thought about work on Monday. And then I thought about the alien plague eating its way into the Cornish soil.

"Things change," I said.

She bit her lip and turned away. I watched her wade into the shallows. I watched the green water wash the clinging dirt and dead leaves from her legs.

When she got up to her waist, she turned and asked me to follow. And there was something in her voice I hadn't heard before, something that shattered my resistance.

Without knowing why, I put one foot in the water, and winced as it oozed into my shoe.

From the direction of the road, I heard the roar and clatter of approaching tanks.

I said, "We're going to be in a lot of trouble if we get caught."

She held out a hand. "It doesn't matter."

I put the other foot in, and thought: What the *hell* am I doing?

I stumbled out into deeper water and fell forward, swimming as best I could. The cold made me gasp. The water smelled rotten. I splashed toward her.

And then I remembered my mobile, still in my coat pocket, now ruined.

"Good," she said. "You're doing well." She leaned back and kicked out toward the centre of the lake.

I said, "It's getting deep."

There were fresh explosions from the southwest, closer than before. My hands and feet were tingling.

"The water feels strange," I said.

"It's okay," she replied. "Just relax."

I struggled on a bit further. My arms ached and I could feel the tingle spreading over my skin, like a rash.

"What's happening?" I said.

Debs stopped swimming.

"It's the 'plague from the stars' – it's in the water," she said, smiling.

I tried to turn around, to get back to the shore, but she caught my foot.

"It came to me in the sea," she said. "It's spread further and faster than anyone knows. And it spoke to me – it said there's nothing to fear, nothing at all."

I tried to get away, but it took all my strength just to stay afloat. The dead weight of my wet clothes dragged at me, pulling my head under the water. I kicked my legs in panic, felt a shoe fall away.

I said, "Help me!"

But Debs drew back, raised her face to the rain.

"Just let go," she said. "You won't drown. You'll just become a part of it, like I am."

I struggled toward her, got a hand on her shoulder. It felt hot and slippery. Desperate, I said, "I love you, you know."

She laughed, and wrapped her fingers in my hair. We were a long way out from the shore.

"I know," she said.

Hot Rain

Kenji had been betrayed – set up by Jack Finch and the fat guy, Kowalski. And now an innocent woman lay dead and there were police sirens closing in on him.

He tried to lose himself among the pedestrians on the *Avenue Independencia*, but he was sweating, jumpy and drawing attention. Heads were turning as he passed.

After a subjective eternity, he spotted a promising side street and ducked between the crawling black and yellow taxis, ignoring their horns and curses.

Away from the main roads, he knew he could lose himself in the back streets of Buenos Aires. The city was one sprawling enormity of rat runs and boulevards, with no central focus, no clear definition. The barrios piled up against one another, a mash of competing influences and contrasting styles. He squatted in a quiet doorway, panting, as a police helicopter clattered overhead. His heart raced in his chest. Then he was up again, running from street to street, alley to alley, until he reached the *Che Dominique*, a crumbling hotel overlooking the flea market on the *Plaza Dorrego*. He crashed past the reception desk and took the carpeted stairs three at a time, the gun in his coat thumping against his hip.

To his relief, his room was as he'd left it.

He peeled a disposable paper phone from the pad on the bedside table and used it to call his client's lawyer.

"Where are you?" Maria Juarez's dark eyes burned through the low-res screen.

Kenji keyed up a phone menu and considered blocking the trace she had on his call. He didn't want to trust anyone until he knew why Finch and Kowalski had turned on him. But he needed her help: he was a hunted man, exposed and vulnerable. He stepped over to the window and checked the street. Advertising holograms burned above the downtown skyscrapers.

"I'm at the hotel," he said.

She let out a breath. "I'll be there in ten minutes."

When she arrived, she'd ditched her business suit for a pair of jeans and a black t-shirt. Kenji guessed she was trying to look inconspicuous, like a tourist. She even had a daypack on her shoulder.

"What happened?" she said.

He was sitting on the bed, still angry.

"They didn't show for their shifts this morning. When I tried to track them down, Finch tried to kill me."

"Were there any casualties?"

"There was a bystander, a local. She got in the way. I hesitated and Finch shot her." He squeezed his hands together. "If I'd fired first, she might still be alive."

Juarez tapped her teeth with a fingernail.

"Were there any witnesses?" she said. Even in casual clothes she moved and talked like a lawyer.

"A couple."

She took down as many details as he could remember, using a stylus to jot shorthand notes on her phone.

"I'm sending this all through to my office," she said. "They'll keep the police off our backs for as long as they can."

She led him down to her parked car. It was a black 1956 Ford sedan with a wide chrome grill.

"You get in the back," she said. "I'll drive."

A few minutes later, they were somewhere in the *La Bocha* district, moving slowly. The narrow streets were rough and raw, the air prickly with the heat of an approaching storm.

"We know why Finch attacked you," she said. "We received this a few minutes before you called."

She transferred a video file from her phone to his. The picture was dark and shaky, obviously filmed on a handheld camera.

"That's Kowalski," he said. "But who's the kid on his knee? It looks like Garcia's daughter."

With her eyes on the road, Juarez shook her head.

"It certainly does," she said.

She shifted gear and made a turn. The houses here were made of corrugated iron and pressed tin. They were painted blue, red and yellow. Heavy men in football shirts leaned in their doorways, smoking. The clouds on the horizon were black, like slate.

"Garcia's daughter's safe at home, with her father," she said. "What you're looking at there is a clone."

Kenji frowned, lifting the phone up to get a better look.

"Finch is threatening to torture and kill the girl unless Garcia pays him four million US dollars," Juarez said.

Kenji frowned. "That kid's got to be at least two years old."

Juarez nodded. Her voice was tight. "They've obviously been planning this a long time," she said.

Alejandro Garcia was one of the richest men in Buenos Aires. His company used cloning vats to grow slabs of beef, which he then sold as a cheaper, cruelty-free alternative to the meat produced by the traditional farmers.

Maria Juarez was one of his most trusted lawyers and until an hour ago, Kenji had been part of a three-man security team contracted to keep him safe.

Now, it appeared he was working alone.

"They must've got hold of a spare vat," he said, "and cloned the kid from a hair or skin sample."

He scratched his chin. "Why doesn't Garcia go to the police?"

Juarez downshifted as she approached a red light, flicked a glance at him in the rear view mirror. She said, "It's one of their stipulations. Any hint of police involvement and they kill the girl. Besides, Mr. Garcia has every faith in your ability to track them down by yourself. You know them, you've worked with them, and you're an ex-cop – if anyone can find them, it's you."

She brought the car to a halt at the line, drumming her fingers on the steering wheel, waiting for the lights to change.

"Mr. Garcia's willing to pay you a fair price if you bring the girl back alive."

"What about Finch and Kowalski?"

"Officially, he leaves them to your discretion. They were your business partners, and they betrayed you."

"And unofficially?"

The light turned green. Juarez revved the engine and the car rolled forward.

She said, "Unofficially, he trusts you'll ensure they never endanger his family again."

Kenji pulled out his gun and checked it. It was a late model recoilless Mauser and the grip nestled effortlessly in his hand. It felt solid and comforting. There were six shots in the magazine, another three loose in his pocket. Over the rumble of the engine, thunder cracked in the darkening sky. Fat drops of rain spattered the windshield.

"There is one condition," Juarez said. She turned into a cobbled back street. "I'm to accompany your investigation, to ensure you don't do anything to legally compromise my client."

"Fair enough," Kenji said, "but I can't promise to protect you if things get rough."

He slipped the gun into his belt, hoping he wouldn't have to use it. Then he replayed the video message on his phone. The kid on Kowalski's knee was crying.

"This is Grace," Finch said from behind the camera. "Send us the money by midnight tonight, or we kill her."

Juarez took Kenji to a small, smoke-soaked café near the Recoleta cemetery. It was getting late and the rain had set in. The café windows were misted. A young couple laughed and shook their wet hair as they entered.

"So, how does Garcia feel about the girl?" Kenji asked.

Juarez leaned forward and spoke in a low voice.

"He's furious. He loves his daughter, but the idea of a clone is driving him crazy. He resents it for making him vulnerable, but he's also unable to turn his back on it, as it's his flesh and blood."

She sat back and sipped her coffee. They were near the back of the room, at a table by the wall.

"Besides," she continued, "he's standing for congress this year, and he's always portrayed himself as a family man. If he walks away from this, and the news channels get hold of it, it could destroy him politically."

Kenji stirred his tea. "So, he'd like this whole affair wrapped up as quickly and quietly as possible?"

Juarez didn't look happy. "That's about the size of it."

Kenji scratched his head. The gun felt cold, heavy and awkward in his belt.

"It's not going to be easy to find them," he said. "After our run-in this afternoon, they'll be keeping their heads low, avoiding their usual haunts."

Juarez dug in her pocket, pulled out a scrap of paper. There was an address on it, in Kowalski's handwriting.

"Maybe not," she said. "I found this stuck to Kowalski's desk calendar. He'll be there from eleven."

Kenji looked at the address on the paper: it was a downtown strip joint, strictly members only.

"I know the place," he said. He checked the clock on the bare brick wall – they had an hour to kill until eleven.

"Do you want to get something to eat?" Juarez asked.

Kenji liked her. They'd worked well together over the last couple of years.

"I'm not hungry," he said.

Her phone rang. She answered it, and then passed it across the table.

"Mr. Garcia would like to speak to you," she said.

Alejandro Garcia had a greying moustache and a complexion like weathered marble. He was sitting at a desk, wearing a white cotton shirt and a single diamond earring.

"Hello, Mr. Shiraki. I trust you're making progress?"

Kenji looked at Juarez. "We're working on a lead," he said.

Garcia nodded. "That's good. Now tell me, are you experiencing any nausea or giddiness?"

Kenji narrowed his eyes. "Why do you ask?"

On the phone's little screen, the other man brought his hands together and steepled his fingers. "Have you ever heard of a parasite by the name of *Toxoplasma gondii*, Mr. Shiraki? It's a most unpleasant little beast, I'm afraid. It's most commonly found in rats. It makes them unafraid of cats."

"Unafraid?"

"Reckless, even. It wants the rat to get eaten, you see, so it can infect the cat."

Kenji wrinkled his nose and glanced around the half-empty café. On the screen, Garcia's eyes grew hard and dark, like cooling steel.

"Mister Shiraki, the cup of tea you were given contained a specially tailored cocktail of hormones and dopamine, designed to produce the same effect in you."

He waited a beat, watching Kenji's reaction, and then continued.

"Your former colleagues have threatened to kill my daughter's clone at midnight tonight. If you manage to find her in time, I'll supply you with an antidote. If you fail, then like the rat you'll become increasingly reckless and suicidal, looking for trouble. By one o'clock, one way or another, you'll most likely be dead."

Kenji pushed his half-finished tea away.

"This poison's already in me?" he said.

The other man nodded.

"Think of it as an incentive."

Garcia broke the connection, leaving Kenji staring at a blank display. He looked over at Juarez. Down the street, through the rain, a church bell rang the hour.

"What are you going to do?" she asked.

They took the car downtown. The streets smelled of carbon monoxide and cigarette smoke. Juarez drove, turning the big wheel with her small hands. In the passenger seat, Kenji leaned his head against the window, listening to the thud of the wipers.

"For what it was worth," Juarez said, "I'm sorry."

They were crossing an elegant Italian-style piazza at the end of a wide, tree-lined boulevard. Three-dimensional projections of brightly-dressed tango dancers stepped and swaggered above the buildings. Kenji watched them strut, watched the continuous play of tacky advertisements on their traditional sequinned costumes.

126

A few turns beyond the square, they pulled up in front of the strip club. Juarez had a matt black Colt automatic in the glove box. She held it awkwardly, unsure where to point it. He put a steadying hand on her arm.

"Stay here," he said.

He splashed across the road. There was a man on the door, a local. He was big, but Kenji didn't stop.

"I want to see Tony Caldera," he said.

Inside, the club was deserted. As Kenji pushed through the door a couple of bored, surgically-enhanced dancers eyed him from the stage. Tony Caldera, the club's owner fluttered toward him in an ill-fitting suit.

"Mr. Shiraki! So nice to see you! What's your pleasure?"

Kenji gave him a look. "You know me better than that, Tony."

The man stopped. He had greased hair and a thin moustache that lay like sweat on his top lip.

"Indeed I do."

A few years ago, he'd been a police informant. Now he was a small-time hustler with big ideas.

"You look pale," he said. "Let me get you a drink." He crossed to the bar and produced a bottle of Cuervo Gold. He poured a couple of shots and brought them over.

As he put them on the table, Kenji pulled out the Mauser.

"I'm here for Kowalski," he said.

Caldera looked at the gun. For a second, he froze. Then he shrugged.

"He's upstairs, second room on the right."

Kenji took the stairs two at a time, heart racing, and legs shaky with adrenalin.

When he reached Kowalski's room, he paused to catch his breath. The gun in his hand had the safety off. He had six shots and if anyone startled him, they'd get the lot.

From inside, he heard muffled voices. He recognized Kowalski's. He took a deep breath and counted to three. Then he kicked the door in.

Kowalski was tied to the radiator beneath the window, his dominatrix standing over him in jodhpurs and riding boots, holding a crop in her hand. She screamed as Kenji burst in.

Kowalski struggled with the scarves that bound his wrists. His hairy legs were bare and there were red welts on the pallid skin.

"For god's sake, Kowalski – why can't you get your sex on the Internet, like everyone else?"

The fat man responded with a string of obscenities. "You aren't getting anything from me," he snarled. "You touch me and you'll never see the kid again."

Kenji pushed the dominatrix aside, leaned in close and slapped him across the head.

"We're not playing that game," he said.

He felt a sudden wildness. His palm stung from the slap. The Mauser nestled in his other hand, aiming itself effortlessly.

"Where's the girl?" he said.

Kowalski turned away. Despite being tied to a radiator, he seemed to think he had the upper hand in this negotiation, seemed to think he held all the cards.

Another slap got his attention.

"I'm just here to see Tony," he said.

Kenji squatted down, bringing their eyes level. Rain hammered on the window.

"I need to find that kid," he said.

Kowalski's lip was bleeding. He smelled of sweat and cheap cologne.

"I don't know what you're talking about."

Kenji leaned forward, pressing his gun into the fat man's gut. "Where is she?" he demanded.

Kowalski turned away and spat blood. His teeth were red.

"Why don't you ask Juarez?" he said.

Kenji emerged from the club pushing Tony Caldera ahead of him. The hot rain prickled his face. He had the empty Mauser in one hand, the tequila bottle in the other. As he approached the big black Ford, Juarez leaned over and opened the passenger door.

"Have you got a cigarette?" he asked.

She reached into her coat and pulled out a pack of imported Marlboro. She lit one and handed it over.

"How did it go in there?"

Kenji inhaled deeply, feeling the smoke scar his throat
"Let's just say that I've accepted Kowalski's resignation."
"He's dead?"
She took the cigarette back with a shaking hand and put it to her lips.
"You killed him?"
Kenji nodded. His pulse was throbbing in his temples. "I didn't expect it to be so easy," he said. He pushed Tony Caldera into the back seat, and then slid in beside her. He put the tequila in the glove box with her Colt.
Juarez blew blue smoke at the rear view mirror.
"Did he tell you anything?"
Kenji closed his eyes, leaning his head back against the seat.
"The kid's in Caldera's warehouse," he said.

Tony Caldera stayed quiet as they made for the river.
"This hormone cocktail," Juarez said in the darkness, "do you think it's transferable?"
Kenji shrugged. He'd been trying not to think about it.
"I'm just worried it could spread," she continued, "like a suicide virus."
Kenji lifted the Mauser, slotted his last three bullets into its magazine. "It's not a virus," he said.
"Yes, but you know what I mean?"
Kenji snapped the magazine closed.
"Garcia's no fool," he said. "He's not going to risk loosing something like this on the public, not even with you as his lawyer."
The car bumped off the road onto a patch of scrubby dockland. The headlights played across a row of run-down warehouses by the water's edge. Kenji checked his watch. It was a little after eleven-thirty. He shifted around in his seat.
"Okay Caldera, which one is it?" he said.
The other man looked nervous, but concealed it by fussing with his cuffs.
"You know, they forced me to comply," he said. "That's why Kowalski was at the club. They've got a lot on me – they know my operation."

Kenji scowled. He leaned over and took Caldera's lapel in one hand. "Which one is it?" he said.

Caldera shied away. "The last one on the right," he said.

They stood against the warehouse, waiting for Caldera to unlock the door. Underfoot, tough yellow grass filled every crack in the shattered concrete. Out on the water, ship lights slid like restless ghosts through the wet night.

Kenji was ready for a fight. His breath came quick and shallow and his hair dripped with rain and sweat. He was remembering teenage gang fights on the Hong Kong waterfront; a bruised and bitter adolescence spent lurching from one brawl to the next.

Juarez put a hand on his arm. "Are you all right?"

He shrugged her off. "Kowalski mentioned you," he said.

"Really?"

"He said I should ask you where the girl was."

Juarez shifted uncomfortably. "That's absurd."

"Is it?" He pulled the scrap of paper from his pocket, and turned it so she could see Kowalski's handwriting.

"Where'd you get this?" he said.

"I told you, I found it in his office, on the calendar."

Kenji screwed it up and let it fall. He knew she was lying but he couldn't concentrate. The Mauser was twitchy in his hand and his chest was as tight as a fist.

He turned his back on her. So far, she'd been the only one he could trust. When Caldera got the door open, he stepped through without hesitation.

Inside it was dark and damp-smelling. The only light came from the back, from a foreman's prefab office with frosted windows. He moved toward it, Juarez following, staying close.

They passed stacked crates containing smuggled Turkish cigarettes, stolen American laptops and knock-off German porn. Over by the wall, a row of familiar shapes caught his eye – a row of vats. They were the same model Garcia's company used to grow its beef.

Kenji walked over.

Each one had a label stuck on it, and each label had a name. Kenji leaned close and walked along the row, reading. The names were those of prominent businessmen and politicians in Buenos Aires.

"They were planning to do this again," he said.

Juarez was examining a vat at the far end of the row. The foetus floating inside had a smudge of dark hair and his hands were squeezed into tiny fists. Kenji ran his palm over the smooth glass lid. He saw how small and perfect and vulnerable the child was, and something broke inside him.

Kenji strode up the wooden stairs to the foreman's office. He had three bullets and he wanted to put every one of them through Jack Finch's heart. There was no doubt this time, no hesitation. Any friendship they may have shared had died the second he laid eyes on the baby in the vat.

He held the Mauser at his side and walked with no attempt at stealth. His pulse battered in his ears and he couldn't tell where his anger stopped and the effects of the hormones began. And he didn't care. Right now, he wanted to let it all out. He wanted revenge. He wanted to make Finch pay for the unwanted cloned children, for the hormones, and for the dead woman on the street.

His wristwatch beeped. It was eleven forty-five. He had fifteen minutes.

He smacked the office door open with a flat palm and Finch came up from behind the desk with his shotgun raised. Kenji got off a shot, but fell back onto the stairs as the shotgun blasted splinters from the doorframe. Something took a bloody bite out of his sleeve, but he'd seen enough. He'd seen the layout; seen Grace Garcia huddled in the corner at the far end of the room.

He heard a solid *cah-chunk* as Finch pumped another shot into the chamber, and the child began to cry.

"Stop shooting!" Juarez shouted.

Kenji ignored her. He leaped sideways off the stairs, firing through the office's frosted glass at Finch's shadow. The glass shattered. But Kenji hit the floor before he could see if he'd hit his target.

For a few seconds, all he could do was lie gasping on the ground, waiting for the pain in his shoulder to subside.

Finch appeared in the office doorway. He wore a red and yellow Hawaiian shirt over baggy combat trousers. He held the shotgun with one hand, and had the other pressed against his midriff. The fingers were bright with seeping blood. He saw Kenji and snarled.

"Come on," he panted, "don't tell me you wouldn't have done it if you'd thought of it?"

Kenji looked around. He was defenceless. He'd dropped the empty Mauser when he hit the crates and now he couldn't see it.

"Why?" he croaked.

Finch snorted. From somewhere in his wounded gut he pulled a laugh.

"Some influential ranch owners are paying us a lot of money to see Garcia suffer." He shifted the shotgun, getting a better grip. "By the way, what happened to Kowalski? Is he under arrest?"

"He's dead."

Finch shrugged. "Too bad. I only sent him to the club to keep him out of the way."

He took a step forward and brought the shotgun to bear. He closed one eye and steadied his aim. Kenji looked up the barrel – it was as wide as a railway tunnel, yet somehow, he felt no fear.

"Goodbye, Kenji," Finch said. But before he could fire, Juarez stepped from behind a stack of pallets with the little Colt in both hands.

"Don't do it," she said.

Her gaze flicked past Finch, to the office door. Grace stood there, confused and frightened, sniffling into her sleeve.

Finch curled his lip. "Or you're going to do what?"

Without thinking, Kenji reached up and grabbed the shotgun's hot barrel. He twisted it, hard. Finch shouted, and the gun went off, into the floor.

Startled, Juarez fired with her eyes closed. Her first two bullets hit Finch in the arm and chest, spinning him around. The third blew a hole in the back of his head.

She stepped over him as he fell and took the stairs in two quick strides. Her trainers squeaked on the painted wood. By the time Kenji felt able to stand, she had Grace in her arms.

"I knew it," Kenji said. His shirt was scorched from the shotgun blast and he was lucky to be alive.

Juarez looked wary. "Knew what?"

Kenji took a step toward her. "You've been part of this all along," he said.

Juarez shifted Grace's weight on her hip. She held the little pistol gracelessly, almost with embarrassment. Kenji looked at the gun. Then he sat on a crate. His head pounded.

"I'm the only mother she's ever known," Juarez said. "She's more my daughter than she is Garcia's."

Kenji shook his head. "Then how could you be a part of this?"

Juarez tightened her grip on Grace, who snuffled into her shoulder.

"I didn't know they were actually planning to kill her, I thought they'd bluff. When they took her from me and I realised how serious they were, I went to Garcia."

Kenji slipped a hand under his shirt. His shoulder hurt where he'd landed on it.

"You told him everything?"

She shook her head. "I simply suggested we coerce you into finding your colleagues. He doesn't know I'm involved."

"And the poison tea?" His fists tightened.

"That was Garcia's idea – he asked me to put the stuff in your tea, to ensure your cooperation."

The warehouse door scraped open. Tony Caldera stood silhouetted against the city lights, weighing up the situation. When he saw the gun in Juarez's hand, he seemed to relax.

"So," he asked her, "what do you want to do now?"

They handcuffed Kenji to one of the crates and stepped outside to talk. When they returned, Juarez freed him and helped him out to the car, through the rain. She left Caldera looking after Grace.

"I've spoken to Tony – he's going to get us onto one of those Japanese container ships," she said.

"You and Grace?"

"Yes. Kowalski arranged it as his escape route in case things went wrong, and now we're taking his place."

Kenji gritted his teeth. He was woozy and in pain, and she held the only weapon.

"I can't let you take her," he said.

She helped him slide into the driver's seat and slipped her keys into the ignition.

"Of course you can. Tony's got a powerboat tied up on the water behind the warehouse."

Kenji shook his head. "I can't let you. If you go, I'm going to die." He checked his watch – there were less than five minutes until Garcia's deadline. The muscles in his arms and legs twitched beneath the skin and his mouth was dry, his tongue raw.

Tony appeared at the warehouse door. He held Grace by the hand. The little girl looked cold, scared and miserable.

"She's my daughter," Juarez said. "If Garcia gets hold of her, I'll never see her again."

In the distance, Kenji heard police sirens. He saw Juarez stiffen.

"You played me all along," he said.

She looked away. "I only did what I had to, for her." She jerked her head at the warehouse door, where Grace stood forlornly, the hot rain flattening her hair.

Kenji felt a surge of pity for the girl, and a wild disregard for his own safety. If Garcia didn't want Grace, why shouldn't Juarez have her?

"Go," he said. "And take the girl with you."

Juarez bit her lip.

"Thank you."

She handed him the Colt. "You may need this."

Kenji dropped it on the passenger seat. Juarez's eyes glittered in the light of the holograms burning over the downtown skyscrapers.

"What are you going to do?" she said.

He pulled the door shut and wound the stiff window down. His hands trembled.

"Let me worry about that. Just get yourselves as far away from here as you can."

The sirens were louder now.

"What about Garcia?"

Kenji gripped the wheel. "Leave him to me."

He turned the ignition and the old Ford shuddered into life. He knew he'd get the antidote he needed, whatever it took. If Garcia argued, that'd be fine. He had the gun on the seat beside him and there was a half bottle of tequila in the glove box. His whole body shook with murderous adrenalin. He felt reckless and unstoppable, and he wanted revenge.

The Long Walk Aft

It was Kurt's turn on watch. They were a year out from Earth, forty years from their destination, and it was his turn to be awake.

At first, he enjoyed the solitude. Everyone else was asleep in their pods and he had the ship's echoing corridors to himself. But before long, he grew restless. His duties mainly consisted of checking dials and monitoring the ship's housekeeping systems. As the days began to drag, he started looking forward to the time – six months hence – that he would return to stasis, letting someone else take their turn.

The only thing that relieved the boredom for him was eating. The automatic kitchen could synthesize an impressive range of dishes and delicacies – some familiar, some new and exotic. Each evening he would sit in the mess hall, mouth watering with anticipation, as he waited for his order to appear.

He sampled curries and salads, stews, sandwiches and steaks. Each night he tried something new. Until five weeks into his stint, the kitchen stopped delivering.

Perplexed, he consulted the housekeeping program, only to find that the recycling loop had become contaminated – that there were toxins in the biomass the kitchen used to synthesize food.

Without food, he wouldn't last more than a few days. He would have to purge the system and replace the biomass. But where would he get the material to replace it? His bodily wastes could be recycled, but they alone weren't enough to sustain the system. At the very least, he needed a dozen kilograms of organic matter.

He started by collecting together all the leather and cotton he could find, rifling through the clothes stored in the cargo hold. But he was still woefully short of the weight he needed.

He found a couple of wooden bangles; they went into the recycler. There were some books in the captain's cabin, and they went in. But he still didn't have enough.

In desperation, he roamed the ship, eventually ending up in the medical centre. There were some cotton sheets in here that he could use, and he bundled them together, ready to lug back to the recycler. But as he did so, his eye fell on a case of surgical instruments, and a nasty thought entered his head.

He put down the sheets and looked at his left arm. Then he walked over and opened the case, picking out an electric saw. He could cut his arm off just below the shoulder and feed it into the recycler. More would be better, but maybe this sacrifice would suffice. Maybe it would be enough to get the system working again.

He started searching around for anesthetic, but already knew he couldn't go through with his plan. He was responsible for the safety of the ship. How could he perform his duties with one arm? How could he respond to an emergency if one arose? If he cut his arm off, he'd be jeopardising the well-being of the crew.

He put the saw down. He would have to find another alternative.

But thinking of the crew – all two hundred of them, frozen in their pods in the aft storage section – had already given him another idea.

No, he thought. I can't do that.

But the more he considered it, the more logical and inevitable it became.

So he picked up the saw and revved it. Then he stepped out into the corridor, and with a rumbling stomach and shaking hands, began the long walk aft to where his crewmates slept.

Arches

Ed Rico was watching TV at home when his mobile rang. He put it to his ear.

"Ed?" It was his sister-in-law, Alice. "Ed, I've got an arch in my field," she said.

Ed looked at his watch. Alice lived on a farm forty miles away.

"I can be there in an hour," he said.

When he arrived, she was waiting in the yard in front of the house. She had a shotgun in one hand and a backpack in the other.

"Nice car," she said, throwing the pack onto the back seat. There were wind chimes on the farmhouse gate. The night air smelled of cut grass, and the stars above were hard and sharp.

"Where's the arch?" he said. Alice slid in beside him with the shotgun across her knees. She pointed across the yard to a rutted dirt path leading down through the fields.

"It's that way," she said.

He let the handbrake off and they started rolling.

"Is it far?"

Alice leaned forward. Her jeans squeaked on the leather seat.

"It's in the paddock at the end of the track, by the river," she said.

About a mile later, at the bottom of the valley, they bumped off onto a patch of wet ground. Caught in the headlights was the arch she'd promised him, four metres wide at its base and six tall.

He killed the engine.

"Does anyone else know about this?" he said.

She shook her head. "This is all private property. The only footpath's on the other side of the river, behind the trees."

Ed popped the door and climbed out. It was midnight.

"Stay here," he said.

He walked over to the arch. Its sides were purple, and smooth like candle wax. He stroked one, and then walked over and stroked the other, being careful not to step between them.

He found it hard to believe that the first arch had appeared only six months ago. Now there were at least a dozen of them scattered around the country, more than a hundred worldwide.

"How long's this one been here?" he said.

Alice stood holding the shotgun. "About two hours – I called you as soon as I found it."

He walked back to the car and slid into the driver's seat. His fingers drummed on the wheel.

"What do you think?" Alice said, getting in beside him.

Ed stopped drumming.

"I'm going to go through," he said. The authorities had the other arches blocked off – if he passed up this chance, he knew he'd never get close enough to try again.

Alice bit her lip. Her knuckles were white on the shotgun barrel.

"I knew you would."

Ed opened the glove box and pulled out the St Christopher medal he kept there – a present from his missing brother.

"I've got to find him," he said, laying the medal on the dashboard.

Alice touched his arm. "Then I'm coming with you."

He looked into her eyes. Then he reached up and squeezed her hand. "Are you sure?"

She pulled her hand away.

"I don't want to lose you as well," she said.

Ahead, the moon shone through the trees on the riverbank. Ed started the engine and eased the car forward. The tires slipped on the wet grass and he had to keep a firm grip on the steering wheel to stop the whole car slithering sideways.

"Here we go," he said.

*

As the car's front wheels hit the arch, Ed was dazzled by a flash of light. When it faded, they were on a beach, in the dark. The change in air pressure made his ears pop, and he let the car roll to a halt on the soft sand, his eyes full of afterimages.

There was an arch behind them. When Alice finished rubbing her eyes, she dug a torch from her pack and they walked back to it, arms folded, shivering in the offshore breeze, listening to the breakers crash and hiss. When they reached it, it looked the same as the one in the paddock – the sides were just as cool and smooth.

"Where do you think we are?" Alice said, zipping her fleece to her chin.

Ed took the torch and shone it around. There were islands in the bay and dunes inland, topped by scrubby grass. The wind smelled of the sea. The stars above were clear and bright, and there were two crescent moons hanging low over the water.

He crouched down to scoop a handful of sand. It felt damp and coarse – the substance of another world. He rubbed it between his fingers.

"I don't believe it," he said, shaking his head.

Standing beside him, Alice coughed. She seemed to be having trouble catching her breath.

"What's that over there?" she wheezed, pointing.

Ed straightened up, brushing the sand from his hands. Where she pointed, he saw something dark about half a mile away.

His chest felt tight. "It's another arch," he said. "Do you want to take a look?"

Alice put a hand to her throat. "We can't stay here," she said. "The air's too thin – we'll get sick. Either we go on, or we go back."

"Do you want to go back?"

"No. Not yet."

"Then I guess we go that way."

"I guess so."

Back in the car, Ed hung the St Christopher medal from the rear view mirror. He felt light-headed and tired.

"Are you ready for this?" he said. He turned the key and it took him two attempts to start the engine.

Alice drew her knees up and closed her eyes.

"As ready as I'll ever be."

The second arch took them into daylight. They were in a desert, beneath an angry red sun, on a road made of packed sand. Thin sidewinders of dust skittered across it in the hot, dry air.

Ed reached for his shades. He could breathe again, and there was a fork ahead. The road branched, and then branched again. And each branch led to another arch.

"Four of them," he said. But three were damaged, toppled and twisted by the shifting sands. Only one remained upright.

He slowed down, feeling himself start to sweat. The road ahead shimmered.

Alice pulled her fleece off. She had a t-shirt underneath.

"And that's not all," she said. Up ahead, there was a vehicle at the side of the road, a ruggedly built tractor with fat mesh tires and a transparent bubble for a cab.

"What the hell's that?" Ed said. He'd never seen anything like it.

There was a girl crouching by one of the tractor's wheels. She stood as they approached, wiping her hands on a rag.

Ed wound his window down.

"Having trouble?" he said.

She came over.

"Am I glad to see you!" she said, and Ed couldn't help but notice her accent.

"Are you American?" he asked.

She smiled. "I'm from Iowa. What about you? You're British, right?"

Ed stuck his hand out.

"My name's Ed," he said.

She finished wiping her fingers and stuffed the rag in her back pocket, then shook his hand with a firm grip.

"Kristen. Kristen Cole."

She looked back at her vehicle. "The drive unit's completely dead," she said.

"Can we give you a lift?"

"Just let me get my stuff together."

She leaned into the vehicle's transparent cab and pulled out a rucksack.

"Thanks for coming by," she said, emerging.

Alice moved the shotgun and Kristen slid into the back seat, behind Ed.

"Have you been here long?" Alice said.

Kristen stretched.

"A few days," she said. "Maybe a week."

"Are you on your own?" Ed asked.

Kristen hugged the rucksack to her chest. "I got separated from the others – the people I was travelling with," she said. "We're a research team from Iowa State. They went on ahead."

"They left you here?"

"I don't think they realised I wasn't following."

She sniffed the air.

"Say, does this car *really* run on petrol?"

Ed ignored her. He leaned forward over the steering wheel, looking through the heat shimmering off the car's hood. Ahead, there were tire tracks leading to the arch on the far left.

"Your friends must've gone that way," he said, pointing. "Do you want to follow them?"

Kristen frowned. "Of course – What other choice do we have?"

Alice said, "We could take you back."

"That's not even funny."

Alice frowned. "It wasn't supposed to be."

Kristen shook her head. "Don't you know where you are? Weren't you briefed at all?"

Ed undid his seatbelt and slid around to face her.

"No one briefed us," he said. "We came through under our own steam."

Kristen sighed.

"In that case, I'm sorry to be the one to have to tell you," she said. "But there's no point in trying to get back to Earth."

"Why not?"

Kristen looked away.

"Because they're all dead," she said quietly.

Alice leaned forward.

"Who's dead?"

Kristen closed her eyes. She wiped a black curl from her forehead.

"Everyone's dead," she said, "everyone we know."

"I can't believe nobody told you," she said.

They were out of the car now, watching the swollen red sun set. A parched breeze stirred the air, drying the sweat on their faces.

Alice folded her arms. "I still don't get it," she said.

Kristen turned and put her palms flat on the car roof. Her hips bumped against the door.

"It's quite simple," she said. "Each arch leads to a different planet. This one's about a hundred light years from Earth, okay? And to us, the journey seems to take no time at all. But as nothing travels faster than light, in reality it takes a hundred years for us to pass from one arch to the other – the same time it'd take light to cross the same distance."

"But why can't we go back?" Alice said, frowning.

Kristen turned to look at the sun.

"Because now we're here, it takes *another* hundred years to get back," she said.

She paused, looking at the tracks leading to the intact arch. "It's why my friends haven't come back to find me."

Ed leaned back on the car's warm hood and yawned. He was tired. His watch said two am.

"How do you know all this?" he said.

Kristen turned to him. "People have come back. There were arches leading to Mars and some of the nearer stars – short journeys. They showed us how it worked."

"But we didn't come straight here," Ed said, scratching his chin. "The first arch we used took us to a beach, on a planet with two moons."

"Then you have to factor in the extra journey time," Kristen said. "When did you leave Earth?"

Ed told her, and she nodded. "Which arch did you use?"

"It was on a farm, near Oxford."

Kristen frowned. "I don't know that one. I came through the Paddington arch about ten years after you left," she said. "And I came straight here."

Ed leaned forward.

"That's the arch my brother used," he said. "He was one of the first through. We're trying to find him."

"Well," Kristen said, "if he came through the same arch I did, he'll have passed through here about ten years ago."

Ed felt his shoulders droop. "Ten *years...?*"

He walked around and leaned on the back of the car. He'd thought they were only six months behind Jack. How could their detour have cost them a whole decade?

He looked through the rear window at the St Christopher dangling from the mirror.

"We were only on that beach for a few minutes," he said.

Ed first met Alice not long after moving to London. He'd just started his first job as a taxi driver, when he met her at a press launch in Aldgate.

It was in a hotel off the main street, and he was there to pick up a fare. She was drinking orange juice at the bar when he walked up to her.

"God, don't you hate these things?" she said.

Ed shrugged. The launch was for a new type of phone. It was made of circuits that were printed directly onto the user's skin, and there were plenty of young men and women in the room demonstrating imaginative ways to wear the new devices. Ed had one himself – a free sample – tattooed on the inside of his right wrist.

"Have you been doing this long?" Alice said, eyeing him.

He took his car keys from his pocket, ready to leave.

"I just started," he said, watching the models dancing on the stage at the far end of the room.

"What about you?" he said. She had a press tag on her jacket pocket. "How long have you been a journalist?"

There was a leather bag on the floor by her stool. She tapped it with her foot.

"I'm a photographer," she said, pushing her long hair back with one hand.

"Then shouldn't you be down that end of the room?" Ed said, nodding at the product stands by the doors.

She glanced over at them, then reached into her bag and pulled out a compact digital camera. She pointed it at the crowd and took a picture without even looking through the viewfinder.

The Last Reef

"There," she said, "job done."
She dropped the camera back into the bag and drained her glass.
"Now, if you don't mind...?"
She got up to go but Ed put a hand on her arm. "What's the hurry?"
he said. "Let me buy you a drink."
"I don't drink."
"An orange juice, then."
She looked him up and down.
"You don't take no for an answer, do you?"
Ed put his car keys on the counter. He said, "I'm not taking you
anywhere until you say yes."
Alice smiled, and hitched the bag's strap over her shoulder.
"I'll tell you what," she said, checking her watch. "I have to be
somewhere right now – but I'm free later."
Ed wrote the number of his new wrist phone on a napkin, and
handed it to her.
"I'm meeting my brother for dinner at eight," he said. "You should
definitely come along."

With Kristen in the back seat, they followed the tire tracks into the left-hand arch. As before, Ed closed his eyes – but he still saw the flash through his eyelids.

When he opened them, blinking away the afterimages, he found they were in the heart of a ruined city.

He hit the brakes. The arch they'd emerged from stood at the end of a wide street, with cracked and shattered buildings on both sides. The air was cool after the desert heat. Tough-looking weeds poked through the dusty tarmac. And a hundred yards up the street, two US Army tanks sat poised, facing them.

There were soldiers in the ruins, guns at the ready. One of them jerked a thumb.

"Get out," he said.

Ed looked over at Alice. She held the shotgun across her knees, eyes wide.

Behind her, Kristen said, "I guess we'd better do what they say, huh?"

*

The soldiers were polite but firm. Ed and Alice were searched and cuffed, and then put in the back of a half-track truck.

"Where's Kristen?" Alice said.

Ed didn't know. He could feel the plastic cuffs cutting into his skin.

A soldier climbed in with them. He looked about Ed's age. He wore desert camouflage and carried a black assault rifle.

"Do you want a cigarette?" he said, unbuttoning his breast pocket.

Alice declined, Ed accepted. He had trouble holding it with the cuffs on, so the soldier put it in his mouth and lit it for him.

"Where are we?" Ed said, coughing through the smoke. "I mean what planet are we on?"

"Don't rightly know, sir," said the soldier. "All I've been told is to bring in anyone breaching the perimeter. And that means the two of you."

He lit his own cigarette and held it pinched between thumb and forefinger. His name was Kelly, a corporal in the 2nd Battalion, 27th Infantry.

The truck's engine shook into life and they started moving. Through the flap in the back of the truck's canvas, Ed watched the smashed cityscape.

"I'm Ed," he said at length. "This is Alice."

"You English?"

"Yes. We're looking for my brother – British bloke, about my height, wears glasses... He probably came through here about ten years ago?"

Kelly shook his head.

"No use asking me, Sir, I only work the perimeter, I don't get involved with the civilians."

They came to a fortified camp on the edge of the city and passed through several checkpoints and ring after ring of razor wire. Through the flap in the back of the truck Ed watched the soldiers they passed. No two uniforms seemed to match.

"German," he said wonderingly, "French, Russian, Pakistani..." He looked at their escort, who shrugged and said:

"We get all sorts here, sir."

Eventually, they pulled up in front of a bunker. The guards at the door were Spanish. Corporal Kelly opened the tailgate and helped Ed and Alice out of the truck.

"Go with these guys," he said. "I've got to get back to my unit."

He turned to go.

Alice had been looking at the bunker. She said, "What is this place?"

Kelly paused. "It's the Detention Centre," he said.

That first night in London, they met in a tapas restaurant on West India Quay. Alice wore a green top that matched her eyes.

"I'm glad you could come," Ed said. He introduced her to Jack, and they shook hands.

"Jack's just bought a farm in Oxfordshire," he said.

Alice raised an eyebrow.

"It's not really a farm," Jack said.

"You've got chickens," said Ed. "And pigs."

Jack lifted a jug of sangria from centre of the table and filled Alice's glass.

"I'm trying to be self-sufficient," he explained.

Alice leaned her chin on her fist.

"I love the country," she said. "I just don't get out there much."

"Then you should definitely come and visit," Jack said. "The leaves are just turning, and we'll have the new lambs in a few months."

"It sounds wonderful."

The waitress brought menus.

"I'm going to have the mushrooms and the prawns," Ed said.

Jack didn't even bother to look. "I'll have the meatballs," he said.

Alice looked into his eyes.

"I'll have the same," she said.

Once inside the bunker their cuffs were removed and they were taken to a small, stuffy office where a harassed-looking British army officer asked them questions about their nationality and the route they'd taken since leaving Earth. There was a map of the night sky on the wall behind him. Thick red lines joined some of the stars, dotted lines joined others, and each star had a Post-It note next to it with a handwritten number.

"We get a lot of people coming through the arches," he said, following Ed's gaze. "Some have been travelling for decades – so we're starting to get an idea of the extent of the network. Of course, the relativity thing's a bit of a bugger."

He paused. "Has someone explained that to you, yet?"

Ed said yes. Then Alice asked, "So what happens to us now?"

The officer put his pen down. He sucked his top lip.

"For now, you'll be put in with the other civilians, in the stockade, until we can find something useful for you to do."

"So we're under arrest?" Ed said.

The officer sighed and closed his notebook.

"You're being detained for your own safety," he said. "Now if you'll just step outside, the guards will show you to the holding area."

They were given barcode ID tags, and then led outside, to a large open space with prefab huts arranged in neat rows.

"It looks like a prison camp," Alice said.

Ed looked around. Men and women sat around in the shade, some in small groups, others alone. Children ran shouting and playing under the laundry strung between the huts.

"That's exactly what it is," he said. It reminded him of something from a war film.

A couple of middle-aged French women – one tall and thin, the other short and fat – showed them to a bunkhouse.

"You sleep here," they said.

Ed thanked them and stretched out on the nearest cot. By his reckoning, it was still the early hours of Sunday morning. He wondered what the guys at the taxi garage would say tomorrow, when he didn't show up for work.

Alice stood over him, restlessly shifting her weight from foot to foot.

"I'm going for a walk," she said.

Ed closed his eyes, too tired to argue.

"Okay. Don't go far."

He pulled the rough blanket around his shoulders and rolled onto his side.

Alice and Jack had been married for a couple of years before the cracks started to show. They both wanted kids but neither wanted to be the first to make the commitment.

Instead, Alice got back in touch with her old media contacts and started accepting photography assignments in London. Both of them were restless and unsatisfied.

"It's not like we don't love each other," Alice said. "It's just we don't know how to live together."

She took a sip of wine. She was sitting on Ed's sofa, in his first-floor flat. It was dark but he had the blinds open, letting the city light in. He was sitting on the coffee table, by the stereo. He had a cold bottle of Corona in his hand, a pile of CDs at his elbow.

"I'm sure you'll work it out," he said. They were listening to some classic jazz – an album they both liked – and her foot tapped along.

"Sometimes, I think I chose the wrong brother," she said.

Ed shifted uncomfortably.

"Don't say that."

She twirled the stem of her wineglass between thumb and forefinger.

"Why not? It's true."

He looked out of the window. "Okay – But you don't have to say it."

The streets were quiet. The lights were orange. He watched a car slide past.

Alice put her glass down. She fiddled with the ring on her finger.

"You must know how I feel about you, Ed," she said.

He woke in the camp feeling gritty and disorientated. His shoulders were stiff and the blanket itched. He could hear voices outside.

Seeing him move, the French women brought him black coffee in a chipped tin mug.

"Where's Alice?" he said.

The women looked at each other uncertainly. Then the tall one smoothed down the front of her dirty cotton dress and smiled, showing the gaps in her teeth.

"She's outside," she said slowly, "...with her husband."

When he found them, Jack and Alice were sitting on empty packing crates in a corner of the main yard, by the razor wire fence. Jack had his hand on Alice's shoulder, and Ed could see she'd been crying.

"It's okay," Jack was saying, soothing her. He'd lost weight and there were grey streaks in his hair. His spectacles were scratched and he had a scar under one eye, and a chunk missing from his left ear. He turned as he heard Ed approaching.

"Ed!"

Ed stopped a few paces away. He didn't know what to expect.

"Look, Jack..."

"Don't say it, Ed."

"But..."

"I mean it." Jack glanced at Alice. "I was angry with you both for a long time," he said. He got stiffly to his feet. "But I've been here for ten years now, and I never thought I'd see either of you again. I'd given you both up for dead. So whatever happened in the past doesn't matter to me anymore, and I'm just glad you're here."

He stepped forward and caught Ed in a bear hug.

"You came to find me," he said. "And that's all that matters."

He told them how he'd fallen through the arch that had – without warning – opened in a stairwell at Paddington station.

"I was coming to see you," he said, looking at Ed. "I remember I was trying to find a Circle Line train, so I could change to the DLR at Tower Hill. One minute I was on the escalator, trying to figure out which platform I needed, the next – Bang! – I was lying in a desert, with bits of broken stairs crashing down around me."

Alice patted his arm. "It must've been a terrible shock," she said.

He put his hand over hers. "There were a few of us there. Most went back through the arch, but three of us decided to go on, to see where the other arches led."

Alice bit her lip. "Why didn't you turn back?" she said.

Jack raked his fingers through his thinning hair. "I was angry and jealous," he said. "I didn't think I had anything to come back to."

He paused, and then looked over his glasses at Ed. "Later, the military came and told us we couldn't go back after all," he said. "But by that time, there were quite a few civilians wandering around the network. So they set this place up to house us."

"And you've been here ever since?" Ed said, looking around the compound. He remembered identifying Jack from the railway station's CCTV footage, remembered the sick, helpless feeling he'd had as he confirmed to the police that the grainy black and white figure falling into the alien portal was, indeed, his older brother.

The Last Reef

Jack shrugged. "It hasn't been so bad. They keep us pretty busy. The first few months they had me digging latrines and installing sewer pipes. Then I helped in the hydroponics garden for a few years, growing food."

"So what happened to your ear?" Ed said.

Jack touched the ragged lobe and his lips twitched in a half-smile.

"I'm a canary now," he said.

He told them about the mechanical systems left behind by the ruined city's long-dead inhabitants.

"They can be dangerous," he said. "I lost my ear to an automated household security system that pegged me as an intruder."

"So why do they call you a 'canary'?" Ed said.

Jack touched his torn ear again.

"Because it's risky work," he said. "They send us into the ruined buildings to make sure they're safe, before they send in the archaeologists."

"Like canaries in coal mines?" Alice said. She shivered. "It sounds dangerous."

Jack patted her hand. "It's worth it," he said, "we get extra rations, a few perks – and the side effects are pretty interesting."

He scratched his chin.

"They've got me working in a data repository now," he said. "It's this big computer and you can just sit in it and download the data – Pow! – straight into your head..."

He slapped his forehead. Behind his glasses, Ed noticed little black scabs of dried blood at the corners of each of his eyes, a little crust under his nose.

"But you've got to immerse yourself pretty deeply into the system in order to understand it. It's difficult and not everyone can take it. Some crack up. And so they send us in before they let the scientists take a look – to make sure it's okay."

Ed leaned forward. "You mentioned some side-effects?" he said.

Jack grinned. He glanced around quickly to make sure they weren't being overhead, and then lowered his voice.

"Come with me this afternoon," he said. "I'll get you onto my team, and you'll be able to see for yourself."

Ed looked uncertainly at Alice. "I don't know..." he said. "Is it dangerous?"

Jack leaned over and took his hand.

"You drove your car into that first arch with no idea what you'd find on the other side – I'd say you're ideally suited to the job."

They ate re-hydrated rations in one of the camp's communal mess halls, and then they left Alice there and Jack led Ed to the main gate, to report for duty.

There were three other canaries waiting there for the truck to take them back into the ruined city. When it came, they clambered into the back and Jack went forward to speak to the officer in the cab.

After a minute or so, he came back and took the seat next to Ed.

"Don't worry," he said – "I've fixed it so you'll be working with me."

Ed nodded. He wasn't sure what he'd let himself in for, but he could see a gleam in his brother's eye as the engine coughed into life and they rumbled out of the compound and into the city's maze of shattered buildings, bumping over potholes and piles of rubble.

"Now, tell me about these side effects," Ed said, and saw one of the nearest canaries flinch. The man had black flakes of dried blood in his ears.

"Not here," Jack said, shaking his head.

They rode in silence, watching the ruins rattle past until, after about twenty minutes, the truck pulled up in the shadow of a hexagonal tower on the same street as the arch Ed and Alice had come through.

"This is us," Jack said, and they climbed out into the dusty street.

By the look of it, the tower had once been much taller, before the upper storeys collapsed into the road. Now it was a broken stump, maybe twenty metres tall. There were tents pitched around the base, and armed guards at the entrance – one male, one female.

Jack pointed out one of the bigger tents, where men and women were working at trestle tables, sorting fragments of rubble and circuitry.

"That's one of the archaeological teams," he said.

He led Ed up the stairs to the tower's main entrance, where the female guard scanned their ID tags with a hand-held reader.

"Go to the second level," she said. "They're waiting for you."

After Jack's disappearance, Ed and Alice tried to stop seeing each other, but the shared pain of his absence bound them together even as they tried to get on with their separate lives. In desperation, Alice went back to the farmhouse in Oxfordshire, wanting to be there in case Jack somehow found his way home. Ed stayed in London and threw himself into his work. He pulled double shifts. He took fares no one else would touch. But, with the radio and newspapers reporting new arches opening almost daily, nothing he did, took or drank could blot out the guilt he felt. Nor could it dampen his passion for Alice. Try as he might, it was always there, simmering away.

And so, walking into the hexagonal tower with Jack, he felt cheated. He'd been expecting a confrontation – he hadn't expected to find forgiveness. At the very least, he'd expected Jack to punch him in the face.

"Aren't you angry?" he said.

Jack stopped. They were in a wide corridor with a polished stone floor. "I told you, it's okay," he said.

Ed shook his head. "Not to me it's not. It might all be ancient history to you, but it still feels pretty raw to me."

"So, what do you want me to say?" Jack said. "I've already forgiven you."

"But I don't want your forgiveness."

"Then what do you want?"

"I don't know. Get mad. Shout at me. Do something."

"Would that make you feel better?"

Ed took a deep breath. His fists were clenched. "I don't know how you can be so calm," he said.

Jack shrugged. He still had that annoying gleam in his eye.

"Look, I've seen things in here you wouldn't believe," he said. He paused. "It gives you a different perspective."

Ed let his fists relax.

"How different?"

Jack grinned. "That's the side effects I mentioned." He put his hands on Ed's shoulders.

"Those of us that don't crack up get to see visions," he said.

Ed looked sceptical. "Visions?"

"Strange stuff – stuff that's happened, stuff that's going to happen, all jumbled together." Jack screwed his eyes up tight and tapped his temple. "It's all up here, in Technicolor."

Ed stepped back, fascinated. "What are you saying? That you can see the future?"

Jack scratched at the dried blood in the corner of his eye. "I get glimpses," he said. "Shards, hints... intense *déjà vu.*" He let his arms fall to his sides and looked off, down the corridor.

"But what do you *see*?" Ed said.

Jack closed his eyes.

"I see a lot," he said. "Mostly stuff from when we were kids. But there's also this car."

"What sort of car?"

Jack smiled. "A grey car, a BMW with black leather seats."

Ed narrowed his eyes. "That's my car."

Jack looked away again. "I know."

"And these visions, they happen every time?"

Jack took his glasses off and rubbed his eyes with thumb and forefinger.

"The only way to understand them is to plug in to the system and see them for yourself," he said.

Ed let Jack lead him down two flights of stone stairs to an anteroom where three civilians and an armed guard were waiting. Two of the civilians were men. The third was a woman, and she smiled.

"Hello Ed," she said. "I never got to thank you for the ride."

"Kristen? What are you doing here?"

She jerked her head at the two men beside her. "These are the other members of my group, the ones I got separated from," she said.

She glanced at his ID tag. "And I see you're a canary now? That was fast work."

Ed shrugged. "My brother got me onto the team – he's been here a while."

Kristen nodded. "I know. I've skimmed his reports, and they're fascinating."

She looked at Jack. "But I only just got here myself," she said, "and I'm still struggling to catch up. So forgive me if I'm not as up-to-speed as my friends here."

She turned to her colleagues, who were intent on the trolley of instruments they'd assembled in the corner of the room. Like them, she wore desert boots and loose khaki overalls.

"Okay gentlemen," she said, "shall we proceed?"

They handed her electrodes, which she attached to Ed's chest and temples.

"These are so we can monitor your heart rate and neural activity, and pull you out if you get into trouble," she said.

Ed looked over at Jack.

"Just how dangerous is this?"

Jack smiled. "Don't worry, you'll be fine."

Kristen finished attaching the last electrode and stepped back.

"My colleagues have been here a while – a good couple of weeks – and they're very keen to get into this repository," she said. "But we need you to check it out thoroughly before we send them in."

"To see if it's safe?" Ed said.

She smiled, eyes lowered.

"Frankly, yes." She picked up a file and passed it across. Ed let it fall open.

"What are these?" he said.

"Photos of the first guy they sent into this thing. They tried to pull him out too early and, well, you can see for yourself what happened."

Ed made a face. He closed the file and handed it back. He looked at Jack.

"Come on," Jack said impatiently, opening the door into the chamber beyond.

The data repository was a four-metre hexagonal pillar of purple in the centre of the room. It was made of the same material the arches were built from, and there was a rail running around its base.

"You sit on the rail," Jack said, swinging a leg over and settling himself. Ed followed suit, so that – like Jack – he faced the pillar.

"What now?" he said.

The surface of the pillar seemed to be moving like a thick, purple liquid.

"Just wait a minute," Jack said quietly. "It needs time to get to know you."

"What do I do?"

"Just sit still," Jack said. "Whatever happens, just sit *still*."

He took his glasses off and closed his eyes, his face calm. Ed watched him for a moment, and then closed his own eyes. He tried to keep his breathing regular – he was aware that Kristen and her colleagues were monitoring his vital signs in the next room, and he wanted to give a good account of himself.

What am I doing here? he thought. Yesterday evening he'd been settling down for a night in front of the TV, and now here he was facing something that looked like a giant melting candle.

He felt something touch his cheek and opened his eyes. The pillar had extruded tendrils of glowing material that reached for his face. He jerked back in surprise.

"It's okay," Jack said soothingly. He already had a tendril up his nose, two more reaching for his eyes. "Just sit still. It doesn't hurt any worse than being at the dentist."

Ed watched the tendrils burrow into his brother's eye sockets. It made him feel sick.

"I hate the dentist," he muttered. Then he took a deep, steadying breath, and surrendered himself.

There was a stab of pain. When it passed, Ed found himself standing on an ancient stone dais in the centre of a vast forest, with all the trees radiating out away from him in tight ranks like the spokes of a wheel.

His brother stood beside him, solid and reassuring.

"Are you okay?" Jack said.

Ed looked down – they were at least a hundred feet above the forest floor and the cool morning air felt fresh after the dusty streets of the ruined city.

"Where are we?" he said.

Jack put a steadying hand on his shoulder.

"We're in the repository," he said. "This is the main interface."

Ed looked out at the trees. They were tall and spiky with sharp green needles, standing in rows that reached all the way to the horizon.

"This is all virtual reality?" he said.

"Yes." Jack spread his arms wide.

"The trees hold the data," he said. "Each one's like a separate directory, and the branches and twigs are subfolders in those directories."

Ed turned slowly around, shading his eyes with his hand.

"But there must be thousands of trees," he said.

Jack grinned.

"More like millions – I've been working here three weeks and the forest just goes on and on, in every direction."

He scratched his beard.

"Come here," he said. "And I'll show you how it works."

He showed Ed how to select an individual tree by pointing at it.

"Each branch holds a thousand twigs, and each twig holds a thousand needles," he said.

"And the needles are individual files?"

Jack sat with his legs dangling over the forest floor.

"That's right," he said. "Watch this."

He gestured at a nearby tree and a window opened in the air before them. In it, Ed saw swirling orange cloud tops and giant, drifting creatures like airships.

"Each needle holds a live feed from one of the arches," Jack said.

He waved the window away and selected another tree. This time, the view showed a dark, bubbling swamp, lit by the reflected light of an oversized volcanic moon.

Ed wrinkled his nose.

"But how do you know which one to choose?" he said.

Jack shrugged.

"I just pick them at random," he said. "The scientists can study them properly later. I'm just here to make sure they're safe."

He reached out and poked the window, causing it to break into pixels that blew away on the wind.

"Why don't you give it a try?" he said.

With Jack guiding him, Ed chose a tree about four back from the centre and opened a file by pointing at it. As before, a window appeared in the air before them. But this time it showed reddish boulders on a dusty plain, mountains beyond, and a small sun burning in a clear sky.

"It looks like Mars," Ed said.

Jack leaned forward. "For all I know, it is," he said.

In the window, frost lingered in the shadows between the rusty stones. Ed could almost feel the cold, thin air. He closed the view with a shiver and moved his attention to a tree in the row behind, opening a new window. This one showed a smooth plain like a sheet of writhing purple wax, stretching away to the horizon.

"What on Earth's this?" he said. There was nothing in the picture, certainly no sign of life – nothing but the restless purple wax. It looked like the surface of the pillar in the repository, and like the sides of the arches he'd passed through.

Jack frowned. He opened the next tree in the row, and the view it showed was the same. As was the next, and the next.

"What do you think it means?" Ed said.

Jack shook his head. "I have no idea."

He pointed to the last tree in the line and they were shown a grassy hillside in the process of being smothered by the purple slime. They watched it ooze forward like molten lava, covering everything in its path.

"It seems to be flowing out from the arch," Jack said.

They watched it swallow a patch of leafy bushes, like giant rhubarb plants.

"It looks like it's made of the same stuff as the arches," Ed said.

Jack looked puzzled. He closed the window.

"It must be using them to spread from world to world," he said.

He showed Ed how to disengage from the system. When they came out, it was mid-afternoon. Kristen helped them peel the electrodes from their skin and wipe the tears of blood from the corners of their eyes.

She took them out into the street, to some canvas chairs set around a portable camping stove.

"Coffee?" she said. She bent down and filled three plastic cups from the pot on the stove. Over in the big tent, the archaeologists were still working, sorting their finds.

Jack said, "We found something."

He described what they'd seen and Kristen frowned.

"It doesn't sound good," she said.

To the west, a black Apache gunship patrolled the edge of the ruined city, its rotors kicking up dust from the rubble-strewn streets.

"From the files we've opened, it seems to be spreading through the arches," Jack said, "covering everything in its path."

Kristen looked down the street, toward the tanks guarding the arch at the end.

"Are you sure?" she said.

"It certainly looks that way."

Kristen stroked her chin. "Then we need to know how fast it's spreading."

She turned back to Ed.

"I want you to go back into the system," she said. "I want you to find out how much time we've got before it gets here."

Ed didn't reply. In his mind's eye he could already see the walls of the arches dripping, spreading like oil into world after world, eating up everything in their path, getting everywhere, turning it all into purple slime. First this planet, then the desert world where he'd first met Kristen... then Earth.

He started to shiver. His hands were sweaty and itchy, like they were trying to close on something, and he couldn't stop shaking.

"Hey, are you okay?" Jack said.

Ed pushed a hand up through his hair. He felt cold and his legs were weak.

Jack caught his arm.

"Steady."

He helped Ed into one of the canvas chairs.

"What's happening?" Kristen said.

Jack put a hand to Ed's cheek. "I think he's having a vision," he said.

"A what?"

He waved her away.

"Can you hear me, Ed?" he said. His voice sounded strange and distant.

Ed tried to focus on his face. "My eyes hurt," he said.

Jack squeezed his shoulder.

"It's okay," he said. "You're having a vision, just try to relax – it's a side effect. Don't fight it."

Ed moaned. He rubbed his forehead with damp fingers. In his head, he could see the purple wax oozing out of the arch in Alice's field, covering the boggy ground, spreading out into the surrounding countryside. He could see it surging up from the arch in London, filling the city streets, smothering the buildings, choking the Thames. He saw it join with the wax spreading from other nearby arches, moving unstoppably. And he saw the same process happen in every city, on every continent, until the whole world lay under a thick purple shroud...

He squeezed his eyes shut, trying to block it all out, but the images kept coming, faster and faster.

He woke several hours later, feeling drained. He was in a corner of the archaeologists' flapping tent, in the ruined city. Jack and Kristen were there, leaning over him.

"How do you feel?" Jack said.

Ed shrugged. He worked his jaw, his mouth dry.

"My head hurts," he said, and coughed.

He scratched the flaky blood crusting the corner of his eye. All he wanted was a hot shower. He thought longingly of the bathroom in his flat in London, now irretrievably lost.

He coughed again.

"I'm okay," he said.

They helped him to his feet and gave him a drink. He could taste the chlorine tablets used to purify the water.

Jack said: "What did you see?"

Ed closed his eyes. He still felt shaky and his tongue hurt where he'd bitten it.

"I'm pretty sure I just saw the end of the world," he said.

Jack and Kristen exchanged glances. Jack had a fresh smear of blood on his cheek.

He said, "I've been back into the system while you were asleep."

"And?"

"And you remember that world we saw with the grassy hillside? It's already gone. It's been covered. There's nothing there now but purple slime."

Kristen put a hand on his shoulder. She looked at Ed.

"If Jack's reading the position of the 'trees' right, that planet's only one arch from here," she said. "And that means the slime's already on its way."

"How long have we got?" Ed said.

Jack took his glasses off and rubbed his eyes. He looked tired.

"The images we saw were transmitted through the arches. The slime won't be far behind the images. It could be here at any moment."

"What are we going to do?" Ed asked.

Kristen scratched her forehead. A dry breeze blew through the tent, sending little flurries of dust swirling across the floor.

"They've asked my team for a risk assessment," she said. "And I'm going to recommend we destroy the arches, to stop the spread."

Ed took a step back. "Destroy them?"

Kristen nodded, looking uncomfortable.

"You saw the fallen arches in the desert where you found me. They aren't indestructible."

"But we'll be stranded here."

"I know." Kristen looked at the open tent flap. "And I can't say I'm thrilled at the prospect. But what else can we do? From what you say, once this stuff starts flowing, it smothers everything it meets."

She walked over to the archaeologist's table and picked up a hunk of stone. It looked like part of the collapsed hexagonal tower that housed the repository's interface. She held it in her hand, as if judging its weight.

"But there are over a hundred arches on this planet," she said. "And it's going to take time to knock them all over."

She let the masonry fragment drop back into its tray. Then she led Ed and Jack out of the tent and back into the ruined street. Ed looked at the arch standing at the end of the street. The tanks guarding it had their engines running.

"Why's this happening now?" he said.

Jack adjusted his glasses. "Maybe something's gone wrong with the system – maybe we're seeing a breakdown of some kind."

Kristen put her hands on her hips.

"Whatever it is, we've got to keep the civilians safe," she said.

There was a jeep parked behind the tent. She climbed in.

"Come on. I'll take you back to the Detention Centre."

When they got there, Kristen left them in the compound and they went straight to Alice and told her everything.

She pushed her hair back, out of her eyes.

"Do you know what I think?" she said.

Ed shook his head.

"I think we've walked into a trap," she said.

She took his hand.

"Come on," she said. "You need to lie down."

She led him to the dormitory and made him lie on his bunk while Jack went to find some food.

"What was it like?" she said, fussing with the pillow.

Ed rubbed his forehead. He thought of the swallowed cities, the choked rivers.

"Pretty horrible," he said.

He looked around the hut. It was quiet. The French women – Ed was sure they were sisters – sat on their bunks at the far end of the room, watching the children playing in the dust outside the door.

Alice said, "I was worried about you."

She pulled the rough blanket over his legs. It smelled musty.

She said, "Did you speak to Jack? About us, I mean."

"Yes, I did."

"And how did it go?"

"I'm not sure. I expected him to be angry, but he's not."

Alice hugged herself. She looked at the floor. "So... where does that leave us?" she said.

Ed put a hand over his eyes. His head hurt like a hangover.

"I don't know," he said.

"You do still want to be with me, don't you?"

"Of course I do."

"But you're worried what he'll think?"

"Aren't you?"

"Yes. Yes, of course I am."

She sat on the bunk beside him. "I don't want to hurt him again," she said.

Ed closed his eyes and listened to the voices of the children outside. Some spoke French, others Spanish.

"Neither do I," he said, reaching for her hand.

They were still sitting there half an hour later when Jack came back. It was getting dark. He smiled as he came through the door. He had bread and cheese.

When he saw Alice holding Ed's hand, the smile slipped. But before he could say anything, Kristen burst in. There were two soldiers with her.

"It's started," she said.

She led them out of the civilian compound, to the bunkers where the trucks were kept. The soldiers kept pace.

"The army's getting ready to blow the arches," she said.

Ed stopped walking.

"So, we're really going to be stranded here?" He looked through the razor wire at the ruined city in the darkness beyond the perimeter lights.

Kristen turned to him.

"Most of us, yes."

"Most?"

She put a hand in her pocket and pulled out a set of car keys. She threw them to him.

"I've got something I need you to do, Ed."

Fifteen minutes later, he was back behind the wheel of his car. The St Christopher still hung from the rear view mirror. The shotgun still lay on the passenger seat.

He had the door open. Kristen leaned in. She handed him a water bottle.

"I can't afford to spare anyone else," she said. "Have you got everything you need?"

Ed looked around in the darkened car. She'd given him some food, and he had the provisions in Alice's rucksack, which still lay on the back seat.

"I think so," he said.

"Good." She produced a memory stick.

"When you get back, give them this," she said. "It contains everything we know, all the readings we've taken, everything you've told us."

She handed it to him and he pushed it into his pocket.

"Don't worry," he said, "I'll warn them."

She straightened up. They were in the street with the arch at the end, parked behind the tanks that were waiting to blow it apart.

He looked at Alice. She stood a few feet away, with Jack and the two soldiers.

"Are you coming?" he said.

She bit her lip. She looked at Jack.

"I can stay..." she said.

Jack took a deep breath.

"No," he said. "No, you've already made your decision."

He took her hands and squeezed them. "You two should be together – you should have always been together," he said. "And you would have been if I hadn't got in the way."

He looked up, at Ed.

"Take care of her," he said.

Ed nodded. He waited as Alice walked around the car and slipped into the seat beside him, and then he turned to Jack.

"You could come too," he said.

Jack shook his head. He was looking back, toward the civilian camp. "I'm needed here."

Ed turned the key in the ignition.

"Good luck," he said.

They held each other's gaze for a moment. And then Kristen stepped forward and slammed the door.

"Go!" she said.

The tanks were rolling down the street behind them, ready to fire, as they accelerated toward the arch. The air con blew dusty air. The wheel juddered. In the passenger seat, Alice had her head in her hands.

"Oh, Jack," she said.

Ed ignored her. He could feel the memory stick in his jeans pocket. He knew how important it was as a warning – how it was the only way to stop his vision coming true, the only way to save the Earth.

Ahead, the sides of the arch seemed to crawl in the car's headlights. They were starting to melt.

Ed cursed. He shifted into third and put the pedal down. If he could just get through before the worst happened – and before the tanks started firing – he knew they'd make it. He knew they'd be okay.

He rubbed the corner of his eye, where it itched.

"We're going home," he said.

Alice looked up. "I hope we're in time to warn them."

Ed could feel the car straining. He shifted into fourth and the needle passed sixty, jumped up to sixty-five.

"We will be," he said.

And then they were there. The arch rushed at them. Ed reached over and grabbed her hand, waiting for the flash.

"Close your eyes," he said.

Flotsam

Toby Milan sits at the door of his steel cargo container, thirty feet above the ship's foredeck, watching the sun set. His is the third container up in a stack of six. From here, he can see most of the other ships in the fleet. There are forty in all, all retrofitted like this one to provide emergency housing for ecological refugees – a floating shantytown anchored in the Mediterranean Sea, five miles off the flooded French coast.

Some ships are tied together, linked by gangways and laundry lines, while others stand alone in the gathering twilight, each a separate neighbourhood in its own right, with its own customs and hierarchies. And beyond them, he sees the town lights of Marseille, its downtown buildings and old harbour already flooded by the rising sea, its narrow streets awash.

He leans out of his container, looking down. There are market stalls pitched on the ship's foredeck and the early evening air rings with the hustle of traders and muezzins. Directly beneath him, at the foot of his stack, is a makeshift kebab stall. The smell of sizzling lamb makes his stomach growl and he looks enviously at the customers eating at the counter. And as he does so, one of them pulls back her headscarf and shakes out her bobbed hair.

Shweta!

Heart thumping, he ducks back, hoping she hasn't seen him.

It can't be her, he thinks. Not now, not here.

Inside, his container measures eight by twenty, with corrugated metal

165

walls. Not knowing what else to do, he backs up to the curtain screening off his sleeping area. There's a hunting knife under his pillow and he knows if he can reach it, he'll feel more secure.

But then he feels her climbing the ladder bolted to the corner of the container stack.

"Milan?" she calls. "Milan, are you in there?"

He hasn't seen Shweta Venkatesh in two years. Whatever she wants – whatever reason she has for being here, now – it can't be good news.

He crouches by the curtain, trapped. "What do you want?" he says.

Her head and shoulders appear in the container's doorway. She holds a compact pistol in her free hand.

"Toby, is that you?"

She pulls herself up into the container, gun at the ready, body silhouetted against the fading sky. She's a little shorter than he is, a former archaeology tutor from the University of Bangalore. He hasn't seen her since he left her in Ethiopia two years ago, close to the ruins of a burned-out Reef in the mountains north of Addis Ababa.

"Toby, I need a place to hide," she says.

The Reefs were a scavenger's dream. They started life as simple self-repairing routers in NASA's interplanetary data network – and ended up as something far scarier.

They learned to upgrade themselves. They increased their processing power. They started expanding at a geometric rate. And eventually, they became self-aware.

They were fast, intelligent and ruthlessly logical – but they were also unstable, unable to resist the temptation of further upgrades. Using the nano-scale assemblers in their repair packages, they morphed themselves into weird new fractal shapes. They built themselves extra processors and accelerated the speed of their thoughts beyond all human comprehension. And within hours, they'd burned themselves out.

Toby and Shweta were part of a university research team picking through their twisted, smoking remains in search of useful – and potentially lucrative – new technology. They were colleagues and they were lovers. They were doing a dangerous job and they depended on each other. But in Ethiopia, when a team of rival scavengers attacked the site they were working on, he panicked and let her down.

"I took four bullets in the chest," Shweta says, lowering the gun. "And three of them were from you."

With the sun gone, it's cold in the container. Toby has his back to the curtain. "I got you out," he says. "I got you to a hospital."

Shweta snorts. "You call that a hospital?"

She pockets her weapon. She tells him she's been on the run for three days now, living rough with no time to eat or sleep, nowhere else to go. Still wary, he shows her how to work the shower and while she washes, he fetches the knife and slips it into his pocket. Then he heats some leftover rice in the microwave.

When she comes out shivering, wrapped in a threadbare grey towel, hair damp and feet leaving wet prints on the metal floor, he spoons the rice into a bowl.

"Eat this," he says, handing her a fork and stepping back out of reach, just in case.

Shweta eats like she's starving, shoveling the leftovers into her mouth. He can't help noticing her knuckles are red and raw, and there are bruises on her arms.

When she's finished eating, he takes her down to the deck and they walk up to the ship's bow, where they lean on the rail and look out at the lights of Marseille.

"So, what are you running from?" he says. He feels safer out here in the open, with other people around.

Shweta looks down at the water, letting her hair fall forward.

"It's Morgan."

Toby takes a firm grip on the ship's rail. He remembers Rob Morgan as a colleague – a quiet, serious member of the Ethiopian expedition.

"What's he done? Has he hurt you?"

Shweta shakes her head. She still has the gun. Tucked into her belt, it makes a conspicuous bulge. "It's not like that," she says.

"Then what is it?"

Shweta looks up and the wind ruffles her hair. She's wearing a pair of his old jeans, pulled tight with a canvas belt, and a t-shirt so big on her that it hangs off one shoulder.

"About a week ago, we were scouting a Reef in Thailand, near the Cambodian border," she says, "and it attacked us."

Toby's eyes widen. Active Reefs are exceptionally rare, and exceedingly dangerous.

Shweta tightens her grip on his arm. "It corrupted our suits with nanotech spores. It killed Kamal and Rani. And if Morgan hadn't come in with the flamethrower and the blue goo, it would've killed me too."

She lets go, taking a step back.

"So... you're okay?" Toby says.

She shakes her head. Discreetly, she hikes up the hem of her t-shirt to show him the top of her right hip, where the skin's hardened into something gnarled and fibrous, like coral. Appalled, Toby leans closer. He's seen infections like this before, in pictures.

"What are you going to do?" he asks.

Shweta lets the t-shirt drop back into place. Her eyes are the same colour as her hair. Overhead, the first stars are appearing.

"I don't know," she says.

Toby takes her down to one of the empty cargo containers in the stacks near the stern, where he knows she'll be safe. He uses the last of his money to buy her some food and water, and makes sure she still has the gun.

"Stay here," he says, and locks the door from the outside. Then he goes back to his place and pulls the hunting knife from his pocket. He won it in a poker game in Amsterdam. It has a matt black carbon steel blade and a lightweight plastic handle. He slips it into his sock and secures it in place with electrical tape.

He knows they don't have much time. The university can't risk an outbreak of Reef spores. They'll expect Rob Morgan to bring Shweta in before the infection spreads and new Reefs start appearing.

Toby's seen the havoc a live Reef can cause. But after abandoning her in Ethiopia, he just can't bring himself to turn Shweta in. He knows if he does, they'll kill her in order to kill the contamination.

Instead, he sweeps a few possessions into an old laptop case. Then he's out the door, down the ladder and past the kebab stall, heading for the stern, where he hopes to find Odette.

Two years ago, when he fled the debacle in Ethiopia, Toby walked away from everything – his apartment, his teaching job – taking only his passport and the money he had in his pockets.

Fleeing his guilt, he hitchhiked his way randomly across Europe, sleeping in service areas and railway stations. He got drunk in Prague, Warsaw and Bucharest.

And then one morning he found himself in Amsterdam, exhausted and spent, wading across a flooded street in the drifting rain. The city was half-deserted, everything boarded-up. He'd been playing cards all night above a café in the red light district, and now it was dawn and here he was, feeling wretched and looking for somewhere to sleep, a knife in his back pocket and fourteen Euros in loose change. He hadn't washed in five days, hadn't had a shave in six. His coat – which he'd stolen from a cloakroom in Zagreb – had a tear in the sleeve.

He was ankle-deep in dirty sea water, wondering where he could get something to eat, when he heard a shout. It was one of the girls from the café, a young French dancer named Odette, a nineteen year-old runaway from the outskirts of Paris. She came sloshing after him.

"Do you have anywhere to sleep?" she said.

He shook his head.

"I didn't think so. Come with me." She took him back to her room – a damp studio apartment in a crumbling town house – and offered him the couch. Then she went into the bathroom and wrapped her wet hair in a towel.

"I hate what's happening to this town," she said.

Toby shrugged off his coat and sat down. His feet hurt from the cold water. He kicked off his sodden shoes. His socks were wet and threadbare, his reflection in the dead TV ragged and unkempt.

"Then why don't you leave?" he said. He turned on the TV, found a news channel.

"Where would I go?" She came back into the room, rubbing her hair, just in time to catch the end of a news item about refugees moving onto container ships in the Mediterranean.

She lowered the towel.

"Hey, wind that back," she said.

Now, hurrying toward the ship's stern, Toby doesn't know what he's going to do. He can't hide Shweta here, on board, and his guilt won't let him abandon her. He needs a third option.

Odette's crate is at the bottom of a small stack overlooking the stern.

He walks up and raps on the metal door. He hears movement inside, and then Odette calls out:

"Hello? Who is there?"

Toby pulls the door open. "It's me. Can I come in?"

Inside, there are candles burning, scarves and blankets taped to the walls, rugs and cushions scattered on the floor. Odette's wearing a loose dress under a tight Levi jacket, sparkly lipstick and silver nail polish.

"You look happy," he says.

She smiles. Since leaving Amsterdam with her, he's watched her blossom into a young woman, shrugging off her teenage years like an old coat.

"I had a good day," she says. "I've been over on the *Topkapi*, with Safak at the bazaar."

She looks him up and down. "But what about you? You look worried. Would a cup of tea help? I have apple or sage..."

She reaches for the kettle but Toby catches her wrist.

"It's Shweta," he says.

Odette pulls back and her lip curls. "What about her?"

"She's here."

Odette jabs her finger at the deck. "That woman is here, now, on this vessel?"

Toby takes a deep breath.

"Yes," he says, "yes she is – and she needs our help."

They step out. It's a warm night and there's music from the market on the foredeck. Odette has her arm wrapped in his. "I cannot believe I'm letting you talk me into this," she says.

They walk along the stern rail, past a row of inflatable lifeboats.

"Where is she?"

Toby stops. "Down here, two stacks over."

He adjusts the strap of his laptop case. Inside, he's carrying his passport, a few clothes, and a bottle of water. Across the bay in Marseille, the town lights are shining.

"Are you sure about this?" Odette asks.

Toby squeezes her hand. He's trying not to think about the infection on Shweta's hip. He walks over to the crate and sees with relief that the door's still locked. He flips back the bolt and cracks the door an inch or so.

"Hello?"

There's no answer. The light's off and he can't see anything inside.

"Shweta?"

He hears her cough.

"Toby? Is that you?"

He pulls the door open, letting in more light. "I've got someone with me, a friend."

Shweta's lying on some old sacks by the wall.

"Toby, I don't feel so good."

She rolls over and even in the semi-darkness he can see there's something wrong with her leg – the silhouette's all wrong, misshapen with swelling.

He flips on the light and sees rough, black gnarls in the gap between her T-shirt and the top of her jeans. Behind him, Odette swears under her breath.

"What the hell is this?" she says.

Toby doesn't answer. He's looking at the denim stretched tight across Shweta's hip.

"Jesus, Shweta," he says.

He drops to his knees and reaches forward. Her gun's lying on the deck. He picks it up. It feels cold in his hand as he slips it into the laptop case.

Shweta coughs again. "Toby, it hurts," she says.

He touches her hand. He wants to pick her up and move her but he's afraid of getting too close. Instead, he looks over his shoulder at Odette.

"You've got to help us," he says.

Odette paid for his ticket south, from Amsterdam via Paris to Lyon. She had some money put aside and she didn't want to travel alone – not with half the population of Europe on the move, displaced by the rising sea levels.

"But don't think this means anything," she said.

They were standing in a crowd of refugees, waiting for their connecting train. She wore a pair of camouflage trousers and a thick fleece, her bushy hair tied back in a frizzy bun.

"I chose you because you look like a nice man. And because I think you are still in love with this Shweta woman." She put her hands in her

pockets and hunched her shoulders. "Besides, I think you are old enough to be my father, yes?"

Toby shook his head.

"I don't know about that."

He had his collar turned up against the cold. He was reading a newspaper he'd found on a bench. There were bad floods in Holland and East Anglia, pictures of whole towns and villages swamped by the rising sea.

"Have you seen this?" he said.

Odette handed him his ticket. From Lyon, they were going to catch a bus to Marseille and from there, a ferry to one of the refugee ships. Around them, the other passengers stared grimly at the tracks, holding their bundled possessions, waiting for the train.

Odette turned up her collar.

"It's only going to get worse," she said.

Now, standing outside Shweta's crate, Odette turns to him again.

"What is it that you expect me to do? I don't know what... what this is."

He reaches for her. "It's bad," he says.

From the container, they hear Shweta cough again. Odette pulls away. "We should call the police."

Toby looks up at the fading sky. Out on the water, the other ships glitter like table decorations.

"If we don't help her, she's going to die."

Odette folds her arms. "But what is it you think I can do?"

Toby takes her hand, strokes her knuckles with his thumb.

"Your friends on the *Topkapi*, can they get us ashore?"

Odette shakes her head. "I don't think so."

"What about that pilot you're seeing, Safak?"

She pulls her hand away and walks over to the ship's rail.

"I'm sorry," she says.

Toby hears Shweta moan. He looks back to the crate's open door.

"Can you at least ask?"

He watches her go. When he gets back inside, Shweta's rolled onto her back. Her eyes are closed. He crouches a few feet away and pulls the water bottle from his laptop case.

He remembers the last thing Shweta said to him, before the attack in Ethiopia. They were standing by the tents, drinking coffee in the dusty red pre-dawn chill, and she looked up at him and said: "You know, I think you're probably the best assistant I've ever had."

Now, looking at her lying here twisted on a pile of old sacks, he feels he's failed her.

"Oh, Shweta, I'm so sorry," he says.

She coughs again and opens her eyes. "It's not your fault."

Her voice is dry and croaky. There's sweat on her upper lip. He hands her the water.

"How do you feel?"

She shifts uncomfortably on the sacks. "How do you think?"

The gnarls erupting from her hip are black and rough, like volcanic rock. He can't bring himself to look at them. Instead, he reaches out and touches her hair, brushing a loose strand behind her ear.

"You know, when you climbed into my crate, I thought you'd come to kill me," he says.

He looks at his watch. Time's passing and he's starting to get nervous. He has to get her off this ship, find somewhere for her to hide before anyone comes looking for her.

He stands up. "I'm going to find a way to get you out of here."

He steps out onto the deck, walks over to the rail. Below him, the black sea shifts like a restless sleeper. He can see the *Topkapi* anchored a few hundred metres away, and the silhouette of Safak's plane sitting like a toy duck on the water at her stern. She's an old twin engine Grumman, almost an antique, still sporting the faded livery of her previous owner, a bankrupt Croatian tour operator. Safak's had her converted to run on biofuel, and uses her to ferry refugees and equipment from the mainland, making two or three flights a week, sometimes taking Odette along for company.

Toby yawns, shivering in the cold sea air. He looks back at Shweta's crate. He knows that just by being here she's endangering everyone on the ship, himself included. He has to get her off, find somewhere she'll be safe until he can work out a way to save her.

He looks longingly at the lights of Marseille. If he can get her ashore, they can hole up in the hills behind the town while he figures out their next move.

He pats the laptop case at his hip, feeling the weight of the pistol inside.

"Hurry, Odette," he says.

A few weeks before the expedition to Ethiopia, Shweta moved into his apartment, bringing plants and books and bags of clothes.

"It's only temporary," she said, "until I can get a new place sorted."

She was a respected member of the university's academic staff. Toby helped her with her cases, and then led her into the kitchen, where he'd laid out two plates of spicy chili and a bottle of red wine. The open fire escape looked out over the roofs of Bangalore, the satellite dishes and lines of laundry still warm from the heat of the day.

"Sit down, make yourself comfortable," he said.

She smelled of jasmine. She wore jeans and had her hair tied back in a loose braid. There was a silver pendant around her neck and – when she finally took her blouse off – a tiny tattooed rose petal between her breasts.

She saw him looking at it and touched it with her fingers. It made her uncomfortable.

"I once lost my heart," she said.

Now, standing at the ship's rail, he remembers that night with an intensity that pisses him off. For two years he's been trying to forget it, to block it out. Yet here it is, vivid and alive in his mind's eye. He leans his forehead on the cold metal rail, trying to stop himself picturing the bullet scars that have disfigured the rose tattoo.

And then he hears footsteps. Rob Morgan slides up to him, dressed in a simple grey linen suit.

"Where is she, Milan?"

Toby steps back from the rail and Morgan looms over him. He's tall, thin as a rake. He reaches out and takes Toby by the upper arm. His hand feels like a clamp.

"Where is she? Is she in this crate?" He looks at the open door.

Toby tries to pull away but Morgan's grip tightens. "I don't like this any more than you do," he says. He pulls up the flap of Toby's laptop case and sticks his hand in. He pulls out Shweta's gun.

He pushes Toby's back against the ship's rail and twists the gun barrel into his side.

"I have to find her," he says.

Toby squirms. He can smell Morgan's cologne. "She's not here."

"Then where is she?"

Toby opens his mouth for another denial, but then there's a cough and they both look round.

Shweta's standing in the crate's open door; hand on the wall for support, keeping the weight off her bulging thigh.

"Hello Rob," she says.

Morgan pushes Toby aside. He looks shocked by her deformity.

"You know why I'm here," he says.

Shweta nods. She looks exhausted, ready to surrender. "It's all right," she says.

She pulls herself over to the ship's rail, each painful step making Toby wince. He wants to help her but Rob holds him back.

"I'm sorry," Rob says. He points his gun at Shweta. "I'm really very sorry."

She leans over the rail, favouring her good leg.

"Just do it," she says.

He shoots her in the back. She slumps forward against the ship's rail, limbs shaking spastically. Toby cries out – but it's too late. Morgan raises his arm and shoots her again, this time in the back of the head. She tips over the rail and falls out of sight.

Toby stands stunned, ears ringing. He looks over at Rob Morgan. Then without thinking, he lunges at him.

Caught off guard, Morgan staggers back, dropping his weapon. Toby tries to get his arm around Morgan's neck but the other man twists, pulling Toby off balance, and they both crash to the deck.

Pinned under his opponent, Toby scrabbles for the knife in his sock. But Morgan sees what he's doing and slaps his hand away, grabbing for the weapon himself, ripping the tape free from Toby's leg.

Toby tries to wriggle away but Morgan's thin frame belies his strength, and he punches the blade into Toby's thigh. Everything goes red and Toby hears his own voice screaming. Then the pressure lifts and Morgan's scrambling off him.

He reaches down and lifts Toby by the shirt, the knife still stinking out of his leg. He heaves over him to the rail, where Shweta stood moments before. Below, the black water gurgles hungrily against the side of the ship.

"Do you know what you've done?" Morgan says. He shakes Toby. "By keeping her here, you've infected the whole ship, yourself included."

He shakes Toby hard, slaps his face.

"Now I've got no choice. You've left me with no other option. If there are Reef spores blowing around, I have to call in an air strike."

He grabs Toby's belt and lifts, trying to heave him over the rail.

"No!" Toby struggles. He's seen Reefs sterilized from the air before, with napalm. He knows if Morgan makes his call, the people on this boat won't stand a chance.

"No, you can't do it." He kicks out but Morgan's got him off balance and he can feel himself going over, tipping toward the water. In desperation, he uses his free hand to pull the slippery knife from his thigh and buries it in Morgan's skinny neck. Morgan cries out and together, still struggling, they fall.

Toby hits the water so hard it knocks the breath from him. He goes under, dragged down by the weight of his wet clothes, stunned by the cold. His stabbed leg feels like it's on fire. He can't kick for the surface. Blood curls in the water around him.

This is it, he thinks, his arms flailing.

And far below, something glitters on the sea bed. Something shines. But he can't hold his breath. He has an impression of something black and gnarly blossoming down there in the darkness, and then there's nothing but the roar of the water in his ears and the thrashing, suffocating pain.

Cat in a Box

I sat in the main bar of the Omega Point with a thin man from another planet. He had delicate features and thin hands and his name was Herschel Blake. He was a well-educated hustler and card sharp. And he had a problem. He'd been hanging around the periphery of the Omega Point for some months now, fleecing tourists and port workers. We'd crossed paths once or twice. He knew my reputation, and now he wanted my help.

"I know you've got contacts at the port," he said. He was well-spoken, with a gentle voice that made you want to trust him.

"What of it?" I said.

We were in a corner booth and the bar was quiet. At a table by the door, a group of scaly blue-skinned creatures squabbled over a plate of toasted cheese sandwiches. Their voices were an indecipherable babble of squeaks and growls. The barmaid, Ellen, watched them from behind the counter. Every so often, her lips twitched in a half-smile, as if she understood every noise they made.

Blake shifted uncomfortably. He spoke in a whisper: "I need to get off-planet, with no questions asked."

I leaned back. "It doesn't work like that."

"What do you mean?"

"If you've done something illegal, I'll need to know."

My name's Verne Turner and I'm a freelance shipping agent. I find passengers and cargo for merchant captains willing to pay my commission. If you need to find me, I'm at the bar most afternoons. The staff know me; I eat there, and it's a convenient place to meet clients. Clients like Herschel Blake.

"I haven't done anything," he insisted. His hands fidgeted on the table, like injured birds.

"Then what's the rush?"

He looked up at me. His eyes were grey and tired and I could see the fear in them.

"I won something in a poker game," he said, "something I didn't want."

I waited, but he just sat there, looking miserable. The blue creatures by the door stopped bickering and left. Ellen came over to freshen up our drinks.

"Having a good night, Verne?" she said.

"What does it look like?"

She flashed a sharp, professional smile, swept our empty glasses onto her tray and replaced them with full ones. Her heels clicked on the floor as she walked back to the bar.

Blake watched her go. I snapped my fingers to get his attention.

"What did you win?"

He reached into his jacket pocket and placed a box on the table. He slid it across to me.

"Have you ever seen one of these?"

I shook my head. It was made of a dark metal and looked about the size of a large matchbox. There were precious stones inlaid on the lid, a hinge on one side and a catch on the other, both made of platinum. I reached out to brush the box with my fingers, but Blake snatched it back.

"Don't touch it!" he said.

He pushed it back into his jacket and sealed the pocket with shaking hands.

"What is it?" I asked.

He hunched over the table.

"It's a gambling machine," he whispered. "I won it from a traveller in a poker game."

"A gambling machine?"

He cracked a crooked smile. "You could say it's the *ultimate* gambling machine."

"How does it work?"

He pulled himself up straight. "You wouldn't believe me if I told you."

"Try me."

He took a deep breath.

"The box contains a miniature kitten," he said slowly, "and a radioactive isotope. Whenever I open the lid, there's an even chance that the isotope has decayed, killing the cat."

I frowned. "And you place bets on whether the kitten's alive?"

He patted the pocket that held the box.

"Every time I open that lid, I'm betting my life on it."

There are mirrors on the walls of the Omega Point. Some show simple reflections, while others show distortions of other times and places. The one on the wall above our booth currently showed a swirling pink fog. Small bird-like animals flicked and fluttered through it, throwing shadows across our table.

"The box is coated in microscopic machines," Blake said. "They get into you through the skin."

He showed me his palms, but I couldn't see anything unusual.

"Right now, they're clustered around my heart and brain. If I open the box and see a dead kitten, they'll kill me."

"How will they know?"

He turned his bottom lip up. "I think the box emits some sort of signal that activates them."

I shook my head in disbelief. "That's awful."

He picked up his glass. His hands were shaking and the ice cubes clinked.

"There is an up side," he said. "Until I see that dead kitten, the machines look after me and keep me healthy. They repair damaged tissue and fight off infection. Until they decide to kill me, I'm effectively immortal, barring accidents."

He drank. Pink light from the mirror played across his cheek.

"Why don't you just keep the box closed?" I asked.

He lowered the glass. "It's not that easy."

"Why not?"

He wouldn't make eye contact – he looked haunted.

"Sometimes, I just have to know," he said.

*

We left the Omega Point and stepped out into the street. There was a fresh wind blowing in off the sea. Skyscrapers towered up on either side, their lighted windows turning night into day.

"So, will you help me?" he asked. "Will you get me onto a ship?"

I buttoned my coat and turned up the collar.

"I don't see what's in it for me."

He appraised me with a look. Then he seemed to come to a decision.

"I need to get to Bluewater," he said. "I have relatives there, and I'll be able to send you money – ten times your usual fee."

I had been about to leave, but now I hesitated.

"Bluewater's a very long way from here," I said. "We don't get many ships going out that far."

He stepped forward. "If I can get far enough away, maybe the signal won't reach me when the kitten dies."

"And you'll stay immortal?"

He nodded, and we stood facing each other for a long moment. I could smell exhaust fumes and salt water. I looked into his eyes. There was something there, something desperate.

I said, "What guarantee do I have that you'll send the money?"

He dropped his shoulders. "I can't offer you anything as collateral. I don't have anything of any value, except this box. Would you take it? You're the only one who knows what it is, so you're the only one I can trust not to open it."

I stepped back, not wanting to touch it. "Won't it infect me, too?"

He shrugged: "Maybe, I don't know."

The wind blew scraps of litter around our feet. What did I have to lose? If he didn't send the money, I could always sell the box.

After a moment's hesitation, I took it.

"Okay," I said.

The metal was cold and smooth to the touch, and surprisingly heavy. The precious stones sparkled.

"My life in your hands," he said.

We stepped into a phone booth and I used my data pad to download his details to a tramp freighter that I knew was short on passengers.

"It's nothing fancy," I said, "but it's headed for the Rim Stars. It should be easy enough to get a flight to Bluewater from there."

He smiled and thanked me.

"There's no guarantee this will work," he said, "it's a gamble, but I'm grateful to you nonetheless."

I walked with him to the corner. My ears were burning in the wind.

"There's just one thing that puzzles me," I said.

He stopped. "What's that?"

"The box's original owner, the traveller."

"What about him?"

I turned the box over in my hand. The platinum catch caught the overhead street light.

"If this thing makes you immortal, why was he stupid enough to lose it in a poker game?"

Blake shrugged.

"I think he was playing to lose," he said, scratching his nose. "Maybe he just got sick of living forever, knowing it could all be taken away the next time he lifted the lid."

He blew into his hands and stamped his feet.

"And you had no idea what the box was?" I said.

He shook his head. "All I could see were the diamonds on its lid."

There were half a dozen taxis in a rank across the street. I hailed one and opened the door.

"You can catch the ferry to the port there," I said, pointing down the street.

He reached out and shook my hand. "Thanks. I won't forget this."

He turned and hurried off, hunched against the cold.

"I hope you make it," I called after him.

The freighter lifted off a few hours later. I watched it rise into the sky from my hotel window. I had a glass of bourbon in my hand.

The box was on the bedside table. I thought of Herschel Blake in his acceleration couch, watching the planet fall away beneath him. Was he relieved, or was he laughing at me? Could such a gambling machine really exist, or had he just conned me out of my commission? I'd seen plenty of strange things at the Omega Point over the years, heard many wild stories, and yet I couldn't decide whether to believe this one or not.

And so I opened the lid.

I just had to know.

More quality fiction from Elastic Press

☐ The Virtual Menagerie	Andrew Hook	SOLD OUT
☐ Open The Box	Andrew Humphrey	SOLD OUT
☐ Second Contact	Gary Couzens	SOLD OUT
☐ Sleepwalkers	Marion Arnott	SOLD OUT
☐ Milo & I	Antony Mann	SOLD OUT
☐ The Alsiso Project	Edited by Andrew Hook	SOLD OUT
☐ Jung's People	Kay Green	SOLD OUT
☐ The Sound of White Ants	Brian Howell	SOLD OUT
☐ Somnambulists	Allen Ashley	SOLD OUT
☐ Angel Road	Steven Savile	SOLD OUT
☐ Visits to the Flea Circus	Nick Jackson	SOLD OUT
☐ The Elastic Book of Numbers	Edited by Allen Ashley	SOLD OUT
☐ The Life To Come	Tim Lees	SOLD OUT
☐ Trailer Park Fairy Tales	Matt Dinniman	SOLD OUT
☐ The English Soil Society	Tim Nickels	£5.99
☐ The Last Days of Johnny North	David Swann	SOLD OUT
☐ The Ephemera	Neil Williamson	SOLD OUT
☐ Unbecoming	Mike O'Driscoll	£6.99
☐ Photocopies of Heaven	Maurice Suckling	SOLD OUT
☐ Extended Play	Edited by Gary Couzens	£6.99
☐ So Far, So Near	Mat Coward	£5.99
☐ Going Back	Tony Richards	£5.99
☐ That's Entertainment	Robert Neilson	£5.99
☐ The Cusp of Something	Jai Clare	£5.99
☐ Other Voices	Andrew Humphrey	£5.99
☐ Another Santana Morning	Mike Dolan	£5.99
☐ Binding Energy	Daniel Marcus	£5.99
☐ The Last Reef	Gareth L Powell	£5.99
☐ The Turing Test	Chris Beckett	£5.99

All these books are available at your local bookshop or can be ordered direct from the publisher. Indicate the number of copies required and fill in the form below.

Name_____
(Block letters please)

Address_____

Send to Elastic Press, 85 Gertrude Road, Norwich, Norfolk, NR3 4SG.
Please enclose remittance to the value of the cover price plus: £1.50 for the first book plus 50p per copy for each additional book ordered to cover postage and packing. Applicable in the UK only.

While every effort is made to keep prices low, it is sometimes necessary to increase prices at short notice. Elastic Press reserve the right to show on covers and charge new retail prices which may differ from those advertised in the text or elsewhere.

Want to be kept informed? Keep up to date with Elastic Press titles by writing to the above address, or by visiting www.elasticpress.com and adding your email details to our online mailing list.

Previously from Elastic Press

Another Santana Morning by Mike Dolan

This is a book about magic. It is also about love...and other emotions. But mainly it concerns those moments when suddenly we become aware of the magical aspects of the world, when we catch a glimpse of reality's other side, peering through ordinary barriers, past a split in the sky, into somewhere else, where we might find something wondrous.

...fresh and untried and interrogative... – Chaz Brenchley

Previously from Elastic Press

Binding Energy by Daniel Marcus

Marcus maps out possible futures and theoretical pasts, crisscrossing reality with fantasy, and weaving intricate storylines in the process. His characters are frightened and fragile, facing brave new worlds whilst retaining their humanity. If you want to know what the future really looks like, then look here.

This is Science Fiction of the highest level. The stores ring with authenticity. The language is sharp and funny and unflinching. The science crackles – Michael Blumlein, World Fantasy Award finalist

For further information visit:
www.elasticpress.com

Out Now from Elastic Press

The Turing Test by Chris Beckett

These fourteen stories, among other things, contain robots, alien planets, genetic manipulation and virtual reality, but their centre focuses on individuals rather than technology, and how they deal with love and loneliness, authenticity, reality and what it really means to be human.

With an introduction from Alistair Reynolds.

Forthcoming from Elastic Press

Subtle Edens edited by Allen Ashley

In this anthology, award-winning editor Allen Ashley has collected 21 brand new Slipstream stories from across the globe from both established and up and coming writers. This is the fiction to thrill, puzzle, excite and disturb. You have nothing to lose but your preconceptions. Featuring stories by: Nina Allan, Neil Ayres, Daniel Bennett, Scott Brendel, Toiya Kristen Finley, Gary Fry, Jeff Gardiner, Ari Goelman, D. W. Green, S. J. Hirons, Joel Lane, Josh McDonald, Mike O'Driscoll, Marion Pitman, Kate Robinson, Ian Shoebridge, David Sutton, Steve Rasnic Tem, Richard Thieme, Douglas Thompson, Andrew Tisbert, and Aliya Whiteley.

For further information visit:
www.elasticpress.com